I looked at my reflection in the mirror. Boy, was I a mess! My first airplane trip had turned into a disaster. I looked down at the stains on my blouse.

Could I help it if I got dizzy and had to grab onto something for support? How did I know the first thing I'd grab would be my food tray? I took a paper towel and tried cleaning off the stain with liquid soap.

Then I heard the pilot announce that we would be landing soon. I quickly slid the latch open on the bathroom door, but nothing happened. The door didn't budge. I tried again. Still nothing. I kicked the door and screamed. No one answered.

"Please help me!" I yelled. "Somebody get me out of here!"

The KLUTZ is Back!

by Alida E. Young

To Betty Young and Lillian Benjamin—
two very special people

My thanks to Domino's Pizza and
Tease Shirts of Yucca Valley, California

Published by Willowisp Press, Inc.
401 E. Wilson Bridge Road, Worthington, Ohio 43085

Printed in the United States of America

10 9 8 7 6 5 4 3 2

ISBN 0-87406-477-5

One

HAVE you ever been so nervous that your hands get all damp and clammy, and your stomach feels as if it's gone down the garbage disposal?

Well, the feeling gets even worse when you're both nervous *and* excited—like I am now. I'm excited because in just four weeks I'm going to New York for the finals of the Vargas Girl Contest.

To fill you in on all the news, Carla Townsend (her dad's the mayor) and I both entered the contest to be the star of TV commercials for the Victoria Vargas Schools of Modeling and Self-Improvement. I competed against Carla and other girls from the western states—and I won! Can you believe it?

And I'm especially thrilled that the finals are in New York, because that means I'll get to see my dad for the first time in a year. Soon

5

after he and my mom divorced, he accepted a job in New York and moved away. I've really missed my dad a lot, but I am nervous about seeing him.

And whenever I get nervous, I'm a walking disaster. I could probably destroy the whole town of San Angelo—maybe all of California—maybe the planet—maybe even the universe! That's me, Megan Steele, Super Klutz.

I figured if my friends came with me to the contest finals, maybe I wouldn't be as nervous. So we're trying like crazy to raise enough money for all six of us to fly to New York together. My ticket's free, but that leaves five that we have to buy.

I woke up early Saturday morning, because Helen Mae Vorchek and Carla were coming over to bake cakes for a bake sale. Helen Mae knocked on the kitchen door at exactly 7:00. I saw that her arms were full of bags.

"Whew!" she said as she set the bags on the counter and grinned. "Next time we do the baking at my house."

Helen Mae is my best friend in the whole world. We do almost everything together. We're both fourteen and five foot six. But we don't look anything alike. She has reddish-brown hair and green eyes. I have ordinary, light brown hair and hazel eyes. Sometimes, people say I'm cute, but I'm not really pretty. I guess cute and likeable are the qualities the Vargas people are looking for.

Helen Mae is easygoing and everyone likes her. We usually get along great. The only fights we've ever had were because of Carla.

"Where's Carla?" Helen Mae asked. I had been wondering the same thing. It's funny, but sometimes Helen Mae seems to know exactly what I'm thinking. I guess that's how good friends are.

"You know Carla. She's always late," I said. *It's her way of getting out of work,* I thought.

"That's okay. Three people in a kitchen are too many anyway," Helen Mae added. Sometimes it amazed me that she could be so understanding about things, especially where Carla was concerned.

Helen Mae set out all of the ingredients for her German chocolate cake. I had decided to make my dad's favorite—a white cake with strawberry foam frosting. We each poured our ingredients into bowls and took turns using the mixer. Then we put our cakes into the oven.

After 35 minutes, I slowly opened the oven door and peeked inside. I was thrilled. For once in my life, the cake turned out perfectly. It didn't burn and I didn't drop it. Helen

Mae's cake looked great, too.

While our cakes were cooling, I got out the ingredients for my special frosting. I put strawberries, egg whites, and lemon juice into the mixer and flipped the switch to high.

"This has to mix for a long time," I told Helen Mae. "Come into the bedroom and see the dress Trish is making me for the contest."

Trish is my eighteen-year-old sister. She and I argue sometimes, but when it comes to important things, she's great. I took the dress from the closet in my room and held it up to me.

"What do you think?" I asked.

Helen Mae was looking at my closet instead. "I think you need to straighten out this mess in there. How do you ever find anything?" she asked.

"I have a system," I said with a grin. "So, what do you think of the dress?"

"I love it," Helen Mae said. "That shade of turquoise makes your eyes look blue-green."

"It fits great, too," I said. "I just hope I don't gain any weight during the next month."

"And you'd better keep it away from Carla," Helen Mae warned. "You remember what happened to your dress last time."

"You don't think she'd try that again, do you?" I asked.

Helen Mae just shrugged her shoulders.

I thought back to the semifinals just two weeks earlier. I had known that being in the Vargas Girl semifinals meant even more to Carla than it had to me. But I guess I hadn't been prepared for her dirty tricks.

Carla had sneaked into my room and taken in the seams of my dress for the contest. The dress did seem a little tighter when I zipped it up before the competition started, but I didn't realize how tight it really was.

Disaster struck when I had to act out a few scenes on stage as part of the tryout. At one point, I had to bend over—and an incredibly loud ripping sound echoed around the stage. I'll never, ever forget it. It was totally humiliating. But I remembered the magic words. *Keep going no matter what happens.* So I did. And for some reason, Miss Vicky, who owns the Vargas School, thought I was great.

I don't think Carla ever really believed that it wasn't me who turned her in. It had been Joe and Gloria, TV reporters for the San Angelo TV station, who had told Miss Vicky. They had overheard Carla bragging about tricking me. Gloria had assured me, though, that the judging was finished before she gave Miss Vicky their news.

Helen Mae shrugged. "I don't know if she'd

try anything again. But you should definitely keep an eye on her, Megan."

"I will. Hey, remember how embarrassed Carla was when she got kicked out of the contest?" I asked, thinking back to that day. "I guess that was a pretty big punishment for her. She's so used to getting her way with everything. It seems weird to me that she would even want to come with all of us to New York."

I started to hang up the dress, wishing I had a lock on the closet door to keep Carla out.

"Yeah, I've been wondering about that, too. She's been really friendly ever since she was kicked out of the contest," Helen Mae pointed out. "It's not like her to be so nice. I wonder if she's up to something, or if she's finally learned her lesson?"

"Who's learned a lesson?"

I swung around to see Carla standing in the doorway. I wondered how much she had heard. I didn't need any more hard feelings where she was concerned.

"Your mom is out working in the garden. She told me that I'd probably find you in here," Carla said. "So, who has learned a lesson?"

My mind went blank. I couldn't think of a thing to say. I glanced over at Helen Mae and hoped she could think up a quick lie.

"Oh, uh, we were just talking about one of the kids who takes piano lessons from my dad," Helen Mae said.

"Yeah, that's right," I added.

Carla looked from Helen Mae to me. "So you don't want to tell me, huh? Okay, forget it," she said. "Is that your dress for the contest?"

"Yes, but it's not finished yet. Trish is making it for me," I said proudly.

"Oh, I wondered why it looked so...homemade," Carla said. She made *homemade* sound like a disgusting word.

I bit my tongue so I wouldn't say something nasty. Carla and I used to be pretty good friends, but we hadn't been getting along too well lately. The dress incident didn't help things. And I guess we didn't have as much in common anymore. But I wasn't going to let our deteriorating friendship bother me. It never seemed to bother Carla.

But what if Carla was right about the dress? My stomach knotted up. Maybe the dress would look homemade even after it was finished.

Megan Steele just arrived at the contest in a tacky, turquoise-blue dress. She looks like Cinderella before the fairy godmother turned

11

her into a princess. Rumors are spreading through the contest hall that the dress came from a rummage sale!

As if she could tell what I was thinking, Helen Mae said, "You're going to look beautiful in your dress." Then she looked at her watch. "Hey, let's go finish the frosting so we can take the cakes to the bake sale."

"Yeah, I forgot all about the frosting," I admitted. I was glad to get out of my bedroom and get Carla away from the dress. "Why didn't you bring anything to bake?" I asked Carla.

"Because my mom thinks bake sales are dumb," Carla explained. "She gave me ten dollars to donate instead of food."

"Money is just as good," Helen Mae said. "But I think it's more fun to bake."

We went back to the kitchen. We stopped in our tracks as we reached the doorway. The kitchen looked like the wackiest, craziest fun house I'd ever seen.

The mixer was spinning around and around. At every turn it sprayed pink foam frosting on the ceiling, the walls, and the cabinets. I raced to the mixer. But wouldn't you know it, before I could turn it off, Mom and Trish walked into the kitchen. Mom was wearing her gardening gloves, and Trish was still in her nightgown. The mixer gave one last sweep around and sprayed all of us.

One big, pink glob splatted on Carla's head and slowly dribbled down her cheek. I started laughing and couldn't stop.

"You look so funny, Carla," I gasped.

Carla glared at me.

"Megan, how could you have let this happen?" Mom asked.

"What do you mean, Mom? Megan has turned klutziness into an art," Trish said. "She gets better and better all the time."

Then some frosting plopped from the ceiling onto my face, and everybody burst out laughing. The scene was so ridiculous that even Mom and Trish had to laugh. Even Carla giggled. We all finally collapsed onto the chairs at the table.

"Ooh," I groaned. "My stomach hurts from laughing."

Mom sighed. She rested her head in her hands. I couldn't tell if she was tired or mad at me for being such a klutz. Then I glanced up at the ceiling and watched as a glop of pink frosting fell right on my mother's arm. Suddenly, it didn't seem so funny anymore.

"Mom, I'm sorry about this mess," I told her.

Helen Mae looked around the room. "Yuck!

It's going to take an hour to clean up this place."

"You go ahead and frost the cakes with what's left," I told her. "I'll start cleaning up before this stuff dries."

"Maybe the next time you want a pink kitchen, you should try paint," Carla suggested. "I'm going home to wash my hair."

"Okay, we'll see you at the bake sale," I said. "I'm sorry about your hair."

"I know you're sorry, but you keep right on doing stupid things," Carla said as she walked out the door.

I had to admit Carla was right. Every time I think I'm through being a klutz, something dumb happens. It's not always my fault. But this time I couldn't blame the incredible icing attack on anyone but me.

Am I doomed to be a klutz forever?

Two

FIVE of my friends and I were sitting at our usual table at the back of Yokomura's Pizza Palace. It was Saturday night, and we were counting the money we'd made at the bake sale.

"Could we have another pizza over here?" I called to Mr. Yokomura. "This time with anchovies."

"Anchovies!" Carla whined. "I hate anchovies."

Carla never liked anything anybody else did. I think she enjoyed driving us all crazy. I wasn't excited about having little fish on my pizza either, but I knew that Andy, Chris, and Helen Mae all loved them.

"I want a cheeseburger and fries," Spud Walters said. Spud's parents own the San Angelo Motel.

"You've already had five pieces of pizza," Carla said, giving him a disgusted look.

"It's used for brain power," Spud told her.

"Well, so far the only ways we've thought of to make money are the bake sale and a car wash," Andy Gerritson said. "Those ideas alone aren't going to pay anybody's way to New York."

"Well, then we have to think some more, because I need you guys there with me," I told them.

"Well, we need to have the money for the plane tickets by a week from Monday," Chris Rhodes said. "That's when the cheaper airfares expire."

Chris doesn't really have to worry much about money, because his family is really rich. But Chris always helps us whenever we need him.

"Well, we could sit Carla on the wing of the plane," Spud suggested. "That would cut out one ticket."

Carla made a face at him.

We all groaned. Spud always teased Carla, because he liked her. Sometimes, they sounded kind of cruel when they joked back and forth, but we knew they weren't serious.

"Is there anyone we could borrow the ticket money from?" Helen Mae asked.

Everybody looked at Chris. The Rhodes family actually founded San Angelo. Chris was not only the best-looking guy in town. He was from the richest family, too.

"Yes, my parents would probably loan us enough money for the tickets," Chris said. "But they're out of town and I know they won't be back in time to help us."

"Well, don't look at me," Spud said. "My dad won't even advance me next week's allowance."

As Mr. Yokomura carried the hot pizza and cheeseburger to our table, he said, "I overheard you kids talking about money for your trip to New York."

"Yes, we were," I told him. "But it seems hopeless."

"No, it's not," he said. "I have a good idea."

"Really?" I asked him.

"What about if I turn my place over to you next Saturday night? I'll give the help the night off and you kids work instead. You take the tips, plus the profit."

"Oh, Mr. Yokomura," I said, jumping up and giving him a hug. "What a wonderful idea! But Saturday's your best night. Taking all that money is too much."

He grinned. "Not so. You kids are my best customers," he said. "It's great to help you, too."

"Are you sure?" I asked him.

"Yes. And Andy can supervise. He works here, so he can show you where everything is. But I do ask that you clean up the storeroom, mop the floors, and leave everything spick-and-span. Okay?" Mr. Yokomura asked.

"Okay!" we all answered together. Then he went back to work.

"We're doing car washes tomorrow and Saturday," Helen Mae said. "How about if we make up a huge batch of my famous fudge and have my brothers and sisters sell it outside of the supermarket and the bowling alley?"

"That would be great," I told her.

"After everyone goes to all this trouble, Megan, you'd better win that contest," Spud said.

My stomach suddenly felt like somebody was dancing inside of it. I was nervous knowing that everyone was counting on me.

"What's the matter?" Carla asked me. "You look sick."

"No," I lied. "I'm just worried. We only have four weeks to raise all that money. And I really want you guys there for support."

"I was in New York once, and I hated it," Carla snapped.

Leave it to Carla to say something like that. But I knew she was still upset about being kicked out of the contest, even though she would never admit that to me.

"I'm going to ask your dad what he thinks," I told Carla. "He's great at raising money for campaigns and for the town."

Carla's dad was really disappointed when Carla was disqualified from the contest, but he has been encouraging to me.

"Suit yourself," she said sweetly.

We all ordered Mr. Yokomura's famous double-chocolate sundaes. That is, we all ordered except for Carla. She's always on a diet.

"Pass the ketchup," Spud said as he ate three French fries at once. He isn't called Spud for nothing. There isn't any kind of potato that he doesn't like.

As I reached for the bottle, Spud gave a horrified howl. "No, Megan. Please!" he said. "Let someone else pass it. I can't handle another Megan-the-Klutz mess right now."

I pretended to beat on the bottom of the bottle. "Spud, don't you know that I'm not a klutz anymore? I'm a new Megan!" I assured him.

Nothing came out of the bottle, so I gave the bottom a hit. Spud ducked under the table. Everybody laughed, because for the first time in my life, I didn't spill ketchup on me, the table, or anyone else.

Spud peered out from under the table. "Is it safe to come out?" he asked.

"Knock it off," Andy said, coming to my defense. "Stop picking on Megan."

I smiled at Andy to thank him. He took my hand and squeezed it. Andy is really special to me. He always takes my side in things. It means a lot, because everyone else likes to joke and tease me. When Andy looks at me with his warm, gray eyes, I practically melt into a puddle.

19

The beautiful princess looks at her Prince Charming. He takes her hand. She is no longer afraid. She can conquer the world.

"Megan Steele?"

Startled from my daydream, I looked up to see a woman standing beside the table.

"You're Megan Steele, aren't you?" she asked again.

"Yes, I'm Megan," I said, wondering what she could want with me.

"I'm sorry to interrupt, but I'm Ann Margolis, a reporter for *The Los Angeles Sentinel.* Could I ask you a few questions?"

She handed me a card with her name on it. I had spoken to reporters from nearby towns, but this one was different. This was a reporter from a big Los Angeles paper!

"I recognized you from a TV program I watched," the woman explained. "You're representing the western states in the Vargas Girl Contest. Right?"

I nodded, feeling both proud and embarrassed.

"This won't take very long," Ms. Margolis said. "We could go sit over there." She pointed to an empty table three down from where we were.

Spud spoke up. "Why don't you do it right here?" he suggested. "The reason we're all here right now is to figure out ways to earn money, so we can all go with Megan to New York."

"That's a great angle," the reporter said.

The waiter set our sundaes on the table.

"Would you like something to eat or drink, Ms. Margolis?" I asked.

"No, thanks. I just finished eating," she said.

Andy brought another chair over to our table. I stood up to move mine so Ms. Margolis could sit next to me. But when I tried to take a step, my foot wouldn't work right. I stumbled and grabbed onto the table to keep from falling. I bumped my tall sundae glass. Whipped cream and chocolate syrup splattered all over Ann's blouse.

"Ooh!" she gasped.

Right then I wanted to disappear from the face of the earth. How could I be so clumsy?

I glanced down at my feet—and saw the reason I couldn't walk. My shoelaces were tied together! I glanced at Spud and saw that he was trying like crazy not to laugh. He must have tied my laces while he was under the table. He had deliberately made me look like a klutz.

I was so mad that I could have screamed at him right in front of everyone. But I didn't want the reporter to write a story saying how rude I was to my friends.

"I'm so sorry," I told Ms. Margolis.

I felt terrible. The first big-city reporter I've ever met gets clobbered by my whipped cream. I leaned down to untie my shoelaces.

"I hope your blouse isn't ruined. I'll pay to have it cleaned," I told her.

"No, don't worry about it," she said.

The waiter brought over a damp towel.

"Meet Megan the Klutz," Spud said to Ann. "You're lucky. The first time she met Chris, she spit pizza all over his white shorts." Spud pointed to Chris.

"It wasn't the way Spud makes it sound," Andy spoke up to defend me. "Megan was choking on a piece of pizza. I had to give her the Heimlich maneuver to get the food unstuck or she would have choked to death."

"She's always been klutzy," Carla spoke up. "Even in first grade, Megan knocked over a whole fish aquarium. Can you believe that? There were little fish squirming everywhere. Then Megan skidded on the water and hit the teacher's desk. Papers flew into the water and the teacher started screaming. What a disaster that was!"

Everyone was laughing, except me. I glared at Spud and Carla.

Andy came to my rescue again. "Megan can be klutzy sometimes. But it's not always her fault. And it *is* what put her in the finals for the Vargas Girl contest," he pointed out.

"Really?" Ms. Margolis asked, taking out her notebook and a pen. "Tell me about it."

"Victoria Vargas figured that if she featured a

girl in her commercials who was naturally a little klutzy, that other girls would relate to that," Andy explained. "And the commercials would show how the Vargas self-improvement school taught the same girl to be graceful and confident."

The reporter asked me some personal questions, then she wanted to know how we were going to earn money for plane tickets.

"Well, so far we're planning more bake sales and a car wash," I told her. "And Mr. Yokomura just offered to let us be his help here Saturday night. He's offered to let us keep tips and all the profit he gets."

"What a nice thing for him to do," Ms. Margolis said. "You know, this place has the best pizza I've had in years. I'm going to recommend that our food editor come to San Angelo and try it for himself."

"Wow!" I said. "Mr. Yokomura would be so excited."

"I have an idea how you can make money, too," she said. "My daughter's class raised over $2,000 by selling T-shirts. I can give you the name of the wholesale store where they bought the shirts."

"That's a good idea," Andy said, taking the slip of paper she handed him. "We could put the name San Angelo on them."

"I'll use that in the article," Ann said. "A lot of

people in San Angelo read our paper. I'm sure they would be glad to buy a T-shirt to support you."

Ms. Margolis thanked me for the interview. She jotted down my address to send me some copies of my story when it was published.

"Well, I'm off," she said with a wave. "Good luck in New York, Megan."

"Thanks," I said. "You've been really nice, especially since I nearly ruined your blouse."

"Don't worry about it, Megan," Ann said. "I used to be called Accident Annie. Believe me, I've spilled stuff on people a million times. The amazing thing is that the klutziness disappeared as I got older. It'll happen to you, too."

I certainly hoped she was right.

"I can't believe you tied my shoelaces together, Spud," I said after Ms. Margolis was gone. "Why would you do that to me?"

"Who, me?" Spud asked innocently.

Andy just shook his head.

"Yes, you, you creep," I said.

"Take it easy," Carla said. "It's not such a big deal. You gave your interview."

"Spud Walters, when are you going to grow up?" I asked him.

He just sat there grinning back at me.

I looked down and saw that whipped cream had spattered down the front of my shirt.

"Helen Mae, want to come with me?" I asked, nodding toward the restroom.

"Sure," she said.

I started to walk and didn't bother to watch where I was stepping. I guess there was more gooey sundae on the floor, because I slipped. And down I went.

* * * * *

After washing up in the restroom, I hurried away from my latest disaster and headed across the street to our apartment. We lived right behind our store—Steele's Gallery and Gift Shoppe. Mom sold her sculpture, and Trish and I made all the jewelry the shop sold. I was eager to tell Mom and Trish that I was going to be featured in *The Los Angeles Sentinel*.

They were both in the living room. Mom was going over the store's books, and Trish was watching TV while a mudpack dried on her face.

"You look really weird," I told her. "I wish your boyfriend could see you like this."

Trish is blond and pretty. And she was Miss San Angelo this year. Even with mud on her face, you could tell she was beautiful. It wasn't fair.

Both Mom and Trish had beauty and talent. Trish was a dancer, and Mom was a sculptress. I wished there was something that I was good at.

Then I remembered my own good news.

"Did the reporter find you?" Mom asked before I even had a chance to open my mouth.

"How did you know about her?" I wanted to know. Mom had blown my surprise.

"She called here the other day," my mom said. "She explained about the story, but said to keep it a secret. I told her where to find you today. She said she preferred that you didn't know about it, so you wouldn't be nervous. I sent her your picture to use."

"She shouldn't have met you in a restaurant, though," Trish said. "Every time you go into one, you have a disaster. What did you spill on her?"

I glared at Trish. "My chocolate sundae, if it's any of your business," I mumbled.

Trish giggled.

"I hope your mudpack cracks," I said. "Besides, this time it wasn't my fault. Spud tied my shoelaces together. Sometimes he's a nice guy. And other times he's a big jerk. Why do you always think everything's my fault?"

"All right, girls," Mom said. "That's enough. Megan, your father called. He said to tell you he'd call again on Sunday."

After the divorce, Dad had moved to New York. We talked on the phone a lot, and wrote letters, but I really missed him.

"Is it okay if I call him back right now?" I asked.

"I promise I won't talk long."

"Yeah, sure, honey," Mom said.

I quickly dialed Dad's number in New York. As soon as I heard him say, "Hello. Malcolm Steele, here," I choked up.

"Hi, Dad," I said. "It's me, Megan."

"Sweetheart, I'm so glad you called. You're getting to be such a busy young lady that I haven't had a chance to talk to you in a couple of weeks."

"I just wanted to tell you that I can't wait to get to New York. My friends and I are trying to earn enough money so we can all go together," I explained. "But it's hard raising all that money."

"I wish I could help, but I've had to spend a lot of money on my car lately," Dad said. "It needs major engine work, I guess."

"Oh, I wasn't asking for anything," I said quickly. "I was just telling you why I'm so busy."

"I do have an idea though," Dad said. "On your first night here, I want to take you and your friends to Chinatown for dinner."

"That would be great," I said. I would rather have dinner alone with him, but I didn't tell him that.

"Why don't you and Trish stay with me for a few days after the competition?" he suggested.

"That would be great, Dad, but school starts right after the contest," I told him.

I told him a little more about our plans, then I

couldn't think of anything more to say.

"Well, I guess I'd better be going," I said. "Good-bye, Dad. I love you."

"I love you, too, honey. I can't wait to see you," he said. "Good-bye."

I slowly hung up the phone. I loved hearing his voice, but it made me sad, too. I never understood why my parents got divorced or why Dad moved so far away. Mom had tried to explain about their differences and all, but the whole thing just didn't seem fair.

As I walked to my bedroom, I passed the big studio where Mom did all her sculpting. I looked in. Dad used to paint in there beside her. I could almost hear the song he whistled while he painted.

In my room, I looked at the picture of him I kept on my dresser. I pulled out the big packet of letters from Dad, and began to read them for the hundredth time.

When I finished, I stretched out on my bed and closed my eyes.

Ladies and gentlemen, may I have your attention? We are proud to announce the winner of our contest. The Vargas Girl is...Megan Steele!

Being named the Vargas Girl would be great. But winning would mean even more with my dad there.

Three

HELEN Mae stopped by the gift shop the next morning so we could walk to the car wash together. I had to finish repairing an earring for a customer before I left. So, while I worked, Helen Mae filled me in on the ice skating routine she and Chris Rhodes made up. I used to have a crush on Chris, too, but I had decided that I liked Andy better.

When I finished, I put the earring back in its box and behind the counter. The customer had said that she needed her earrings back first thing Monday morning because she was leaving town.

Helen Mae and I hurried to Anderson's Service Station, where we were having the car wash. San Angelo was a pretty small city, so everybody knew practically everybody. I liked it that way. But Trish always talked about how much she hated it. She said it *lacked culture and opportunity*. I'm not sure what she meant by that.

Most of the businesses ran along each side of the main highway. The station was at the opposite end of town from our gallery, so Helen Mae and I ran most of the way.

"Megan, stop!" Helen Mae called to me.

I looked back at her. "Come on, slowpoke," I teased. "We're really late—"

I stopped mid-sentence as I felt my left foot sinking. I looked down. *Oh no! Wet cement!* It oozed up around my shoe. I tried to lift my foot out of the sticky stuff, and I lost my balance. My right foot sunk all the way into it.

"Why don't you look where you're going?" a man shouted. He sounded mad. "Do you need glasses or what?"

I looked up. A man who was smoothing the last section of the new cement sidewalk scowled at me.

"Get your feet off of that cement!" he barked at me.

"I'm sorry," I said. "I'm really sorry." My shoes made a sucking sound as I stepped backward out of the wet cement.

Helen Mae stood there grinning at me. "If looks could kill, you'd be gone," she laughed.

"Ha, ha!" I said sarcastically to let her know I didn't think it was funny.

By the time we got to Anderson's, the cement on my shoes had almost hardened.

"What happened to you two?" Andy asked. "We were getting worried."

"You're really something, Megan," Spud said. "We're doing all of this work for you, and you don't even show up."

I guess that's the difference between Andy and Spud. Andy worried about us. Spud was afraid we were trying to get out of our share of the work.

"Uh, we had a little trouble," Helen Mae said.

I sat down on a tire display and started picking at the dried cement.

"Oh, no. What did you do, Megan?" Spud asked. He walked over and stared at my shoes. "That looks like cement."

"Well, if you must know, I stepped in wet cement," I told him.

Spud laughed. "You're a riot, Megan! But you have it backward. You're supposed to put your handprints by your Hollywood star—not your footprints!"

I ignored him. "So, how's the car wash going?" I asked Andy.

"Not too great," he answered.

"Well, then, we need more publicity," I said. "Why don't we go to the San Angelo newspaper tomorrow and tell them what we're trying to do? Maybe they'll write another story about what great friends I have and how you're all helping me. That could help."

"That's a good idea," Andy said. "Hey, here comes a customer."

"It's my dad," Carla said.

"Great!" I said. "This would be the perfect time to talk to him about fund-raising."

I gave up on getting all the cement off my shoes and hurried over to his car.

"Mr. Townsend," I said. "Could I talk to you for a minute?"

"Sure, Megan, but I don't have much time," he said.

"Do you have any ideas about how to make money? We need to pay for all of our airline tickets soon, and we still need lots more money," I explained. "You raise money for your campaigns. Could you help us?"

"Well, I don't know," he said, rubbing his chin. "You do have to realize, Megan, that there are lots of other important things going on in town. And there are lots of other causes that are more important than you kids going to New York."

"I know that," I said. "But we're trying to earn the money. We're not asking for it."

"Yes, I suppose you're right," the mayor

said. "Have you tried mowing lawns or weeding gardens? How about painting houses?"

"Those are great ideas," I said. "We did come up with one other idea, but we would need a loan to do it. We thought we'd buy T-shirts and put the name San Angelo on them. Then we would sell them as souvenirs and make San Angelo famous."

"Well, I suspect that most people buying the shirts would be from San Angelo," he said. "It probably wouldn't bring in tourists or anything. But it is a cute idea. I'll tell you what. Let me think about it for a day or two, okay?"

"Okay, but we would have to go into Los Angeles to buy the shirts," I explained. "So we would need the loan pretty soon."

"Okay, I'll let you know soon," Mr. Townsend said.

While I was talking, the other kids had put soap on Mr. Townsend's car. I picked up a hose to rinse off the soap. I watched as Mr. Townsend began to roll up his windows. Suddenly, Spud turned on the water—full blast.

I tried to aim the wild spray of water away from the window, but I was so startled that some of the water went right into the car and all over the mayor.

"Spud, you idiot!" I yelled at him. "Why did you do that?"

"How did I know you were going to aim it right at the window?" he asked, shrugging his shoulders.

The mayor jumped out of his car. Water dripped from his hair to his forehead and down his nose. He angrily wiped his face with his wet sleeve.

"Turn off the water!" I yelled to Spud.

I dropped the hose, and, like an angry snake, it spun around and sprayed the mayor a second time. My heart fell. I knew there was no way that the mayor would help us now.

Megan Steele steps up to the microphone and the crowd goes wild. She accepts her award for disaster number one zillion, a new all-time record for klutziness.

* * * * *

I met Andy at the local newspaper office Monday morning. The receptionist remembered me from the story the paper had done when I won the Vargas Girl semifinals. She led us to the reporter who had done the story.

"Hello. I'm the head of a group trying to earn enough money to send all of Megan Steele's friends to New York to support her in the Vargas Girl finals," Andy explained to the reporter. Andy sounded so mature. "We

34

need help in getting publicity for our car washes and bake sales. And we're also going to sell T-shirts with San Angelo printed on them."

"Sure, I'd be glad to help," the reporter said. "How about if I put a follow-up article in the Friday paper? I'll let the readers know what Megan has been doing since she won the semifinals and how her preparations for New York are coming. And I'll mention how your friends are working to support you."

"Oh, there's one more thing we're doing, too," I said. "Mr. Yokomura is turning the Pizza Palace over to us Saturday night. He's letting us be waiters and cooks. Do you think you could mention that, too?"

"Sure," the reporter agreed. He asked us a few more questions, then wished me luck.

"The whole town is rooting for you to win, Megan," he said.

I think he was trying to make me feel good, but he made me nervous instead. I didn't say much as we walked along the main street into town.

"Why are you so quiet?" Andy finally asked.

It's usually easy for me to talk to Andy. He's pretty understanding about most things. And if it hadn't been for his help, I never would have had the confidence to enter the competition. But I couldn't get rid of the huge knot in my stomach.

"I'm getting scared, Andy," I admitted to him.

"Of what?" he asked.

"You heard the reporter. He said everybody in town is rooting for me. That means they all expect me to win. And what if I don't?"

"What do you think is going to happen if you don't win?" Andy asked.

"Everyone will hate me," I said.

"Come on, Megan, you got through the semifinals without feeling like that," Andy said. "So, why are you getting nervous now?"

"Because nobody expected me to do well in the semifinals, I guess. It made it easier and more fun," I explained. "But this time it's different because I really want to win. I want to make everybody proud of me. Everyone always sees me as Megan the Klutz, and I'm tired of it."

"I don't see you that way," Andy said softly.

I looked into his gray eyes and smiled. He really was a good friend.

"Thanks, Andy. That means a lot to me," I told him. "I guess another thing that's bothering me is that my dad will be at the finals. I haven't seen him since he moved away, and I want him to be proud of me. If I do something stupid, it'll ruin everything."

"Megan, it sounds like you're in this contest for all the wrong reasons," Andy said. "You should be doing this because you want to do it. Besides, I promise you that the world won't explode if you lose. Relax a little."

"Easy for you to say," I grinned at him. "But thanks. I'll try."

Andy stopped walking when we reached the Pizza Palace. "Oh, no!" he said.

"What's wrong?" I asked.

"I forgot to stop at the travel agency," he said. "By putting together the money from our allowances, the car wash, and the bake sale, we have enough to buy a ticket at the cheaper rate."

"What about my ticket? And your mom's?" I asked. "Did you bring them to trade in?" His mom had suggested that we exchange our first-class tickets for coach seats and use the extra money toward a third ticket.

Andy nodded. "Would you mind taking care of the tickets? I have to get to work."

"Sure. No problem," I said.

Andy handed me the money and the first-class tickets.

"Why don't we all get together this afternoon and go over the plans for working Saturday?" Andy suggested.

"That sounds great. Why don't we meet at my house about 3:00. I'll call the girls. You call Spud and Chris," I said.

"Okay, see you then," Andy said as he headed into the Pizza Palace.

"Hey, Andy. Thanks for listening and for making me feel better," I said and smiled.

He grinned back.

At the travel agency, I exchanged the tickets and bought a new one. I stuck them in an envelope and put them deep in my purse so I wouldn't lose them. Then I hurried to our store. The front door bell jangled as I walked inside. My mother came out from the workshop.

"Hi, honey. I'm glad you're here," she said. "We have a special order for a turquoise and silver bracelet."

Mom showed me the design, and I headed back to the workshop to get started on it. It's strange, but when I'm working on jewelry, I'm not clumsy at all. I can work for hours without dropping a single bead.

Before I got started, I called Helen Mae and Carla. I told them to meet at my house at 3:00. Then I got so involved with making the bracelet that I forgot all about lunch. My stomach growled loudly and announced that it was time to eat. I dug around inside my purse, hoping to find my candy bar sitting on top. I finally gave up and dumped out my purse onto the table. There was the candy bar—underneath everything.

By 2:00, I had finished the bracelet, so I got out my pile of rocks. I collected flat rocks that I found near the river. Then I painted funny, little characters on them. Sometimes my mind went blank, and I had to think a while before an idea for a design came to me.

My favorite design so far was a combination of a two-humped camel and a hippopotamus. I named him Guthrie the Camelpotamus. Guthrie wasn't really art, not like my dad's paintings or anything. But Guthrie had won first prize in the craft division of our school fair last year.

I couldn't think of anything new to draw, so I picked up Guthrie and set him into a box. I decided to send him to my dad as a birthday present. I got some wrapping paper from the shop and started wrapping Guthrie. I tossed all the junk back into my purse to make more room on the table.

"Megan, your friends are here," Mom called as I taped up the ends of the present.

"Tell them to come on back to the workshop," I called to her as I finished.

I could hear Carla grumbling as she walked

toward the workshop.

"Don't worry, Carla," I said. "We can go to the apartment in a minute. I just want to finish wrapping this package for my dad. It's his birthday next week."

"What did you get him?" Helen Mae asked.

"I'm giving him Guthrie the Camelpotamus," I explained. Helen Mae knew how proud I was of Guthrie.

"You're giving a rock to somebody as a present?" Carla asked, making a face.

"I thought my dad might like Guthrie," I said. "He's an artist, so he should enjoy getting something that I created."

Carla shrugged her shoulders. I tried to ignore her.

"Well, I think Guthrie is cute," Helen Mae said. "Your dad will love his present."

"Is your dad still mad about getting soaked at the car wash?" I asked Carla.

"Yeah, he was pretty upset about it," Carla said. "He said something like kids shouldn't be allowed to put on car washes. But I don't think he really meant it."

I sighed. "I hope he'll advance us money to buy the T-shirts," I said. "It's our only chance to really make a lot of money."

I put the last piece of tape on Dad's present, then placed a bow in the center. "Okay, let's go to the apartment and wait for the guys to show up."

Carla and Helen Mae followed me into the kitchen. I was getting us some soft drinks when the guys knocked on the back door.

"Great! I'm dying of thirst," Spud said when he saw that I was pouring glasses of lemonade. I gave everyone a glass, then we all spread out around the living room.

Andy spoke up first. "Okay, gang, we took in $63 from the car wash and $87 from the bake sale. Megan turned in her plane ticket and my mom's plane ticket. By switching to cheaper seats, their two tickets turned into three."

"So we still have four more to buy?" Chris asked.

"Yep," Andy said. "But this Friday, the newspaper's going to write about Megan again. That way, people will know what we're raising money for and they'll come to our car wash to help us. We should do better this Saturday."

"Yeah, and we'll make lots at the Pizza Palace, too," Helen Mae reminded us.

"Unless Spud eats up all the profits," Carla said sarcastically.

"Just in case we get the loan, I called the shirt place in Los Angeles to find out about prices," Andy said. "If we buy 200 T-shirts, we can get a great price on them. Megan, do you think you could work up a design for the shirts if we do get a loan?"

"Sure, it'll be fun," I agreed. "What would you guys like on the shirts besides San Angelo?"

"How about a picture of Megan with her foot in the toilet?" Spud asked with a laugh. "Remember how she fell in during the semifinals?"

"Be quiet, Spud," I said.

"Come on, you guys," Chris said. "Hey, Megan, why don't you draw one of your funny animals?"

"That's a great idea!" Helen Mae said.

"I agree," Andy said. "If we get the loan, Spud and Chris can go with me to L.A. to get the shirts. You girls can make up posters and signs announcing that the shirts are for sale."

"Sounds perfect," I said.

Andy looked in his notebook. "Okay, next on the list, we have to decide who works what jobs Saturday night."

"I'm hungry," Spud said. "Megan, do you have anything to eat around here?"

I was starved, too. "Well, we could make sandwiches," I said.

Everyone followed me back into the kitchen and watched as I got out bread, cold cuts, and cheese. We all started making sandwiches. Just as I got a knifeful of mayonnaise, Spud reached over me to grab the jar of mustard. My glob of mayonnaise smeared all over his arm.

"I'm not your sandwich," Spud yelled at me. "Can't you ever watch what you're doing, Megan?"

"You shouldn't have been reaching like that," I pointed out.

"Don't you have any diet food?" Carla asked me impatiently. I opened the refrigerator door and peered around inside. There were two wrinkled apples and several plastic containers with green mold. I spotted a couple wilted lettuce leaves and a small bowl of yogurt and cucumbers.

"Here," I said, handing the bowl to Carla. "Is this the kind of food you're looking for?"

"Yuck," Spud said.

"Thanks," Carla said as she sat down at the kitchen table.

"Okay, guys, let's get back to who'll work what Saturday," Andy said. "I think Chris should be the cashier and busboy. He can help wherever we need him. Helen Mae and Carla can wait tables."

"What about me?" I asked. "How come I don't get to wait tables?"

"I'd rather have you help in the kitchen with me," Andy said.

"Ha!" Spud said. "What Andy really means is it's too dangerous to have you waiting on customers. What's my job?"

"You'll be the oven man, dishwasher, and my helper. I'll be the cook," Andy said.

"Sounds good," Spud agreed.

"Mmm, this yogurt is good," Carla said, taking another bite. "I've never tried it with cucumbers before."

I was glad I'd done something that Carla liked for a change. It didn't happen very often.

"Go ahead and finish it," I told her. "Mom and I are allergic to cucumbers. We look like aliens if we eat any. It must be something Trish made."

"Hey, I almost forgot," Andy interrupted. "Scott Zuckerman and his mom are coming on Thursday. They'll be here all weekend. Maybe Scott will help us at the Pizza Palace, too."

Scott had already been picked to be the boy actor in the Vargas Modeling School commercials. He was the best-looking guy I had ever seen. And he was nice, too. But Andy was definitely more my type.

Carla was a riot whenever she knew Scott was going to be around. She had a wild crush on him and everyone knew it.

"Oh, I can't wait to talk to Kate," Carla said. "I'll bet she has some modeling jobs lined up for me."

Scott's mother was an agent who helped kids get roles in commercials. She signed up both Carla and I when we were in the semi-finals. If I become the Vargas Girl, the contract states that I can do only commercials for the Vargas Schools for a year. After that, I'll be able to do any kind of modeling work I want.

"Well, maybe you could ask her Thursday, Carla," Andy said. "She wants Megan to come over to my house to practice for the finals. You could come too, if you'd like. Is Thursday at 2:00 okay, Megan?"

"Yeah, sure," I said, knowing that Kate was going to be upset that I hadn't even practiced for one second. There had been no time to read tongue twisters and practice scenes. I was too busy trying to help my friends buy plane tickets.

Just then Trish walked into the kitchen. She had her hair wrapped up in a towel. Even without makeup she looked beautiful.

"Are you kids always stuffing your faces?" Trish asked. She opened the refrigerator and started pushing things around. "I know I put it in here somewhere," she mumbled. Then she slammed the refrigerator door. "Megan, did you throw out my facial?"

"Facial?" I gasped. Oh, no. I glanced at Carla, who was taking a bite of yogurt and cucumber.

"Yes, I made up a special bowl of yogurt and other stuff."

Carla made a gagging sound, clapped her hand over her mouth, and rushed to the bathroom. Spud howled with laughter.

"And Carla says I have strange eating habits," he said.

"Oh, my gosh," Helen Mae said.

I tried to keep from grinning. "I'm sorry, Trish. If it makes you feel any better, Carla really liked your facial. How about a mayonnaise-and-dill pickle facial instead?" I asked, offering her the rest of my sandwich.

Even Trish started giggling. "Did you see the look on her face?"

"I guess I'd better go see if she's okay," I said. I stood up just as Carla came back into the kitchen. Her face was pale.

"You did that on purpose, Megan Steele. You knew it was your sister's facial," she said.

"I did not," I protested.

"Yes, you did! I can't believe you would be so mean to me," Carla said as she ran out the back door.

Four

I gulped down my bowl of cereal the next morning so I could get right to work on the T-shirt design. I put my dish in the sink and turned to see Mom standing in the kitchen doorway. I knew my chances for a quick getaway were blown.

"Megan, I'd like your help with the wash today," she said.

"But it's Trish's turn," I said.

"I think Trish has been doing a lot of your work lately," Mom said.

"I know she's been helping me out," I said. "And I'll make it up to her, but I have a lot to do this morning."

"Then you'll have to work twice as fast," Mom said. "Don't mix the dark clothes with the whites."

"All right," I grumbled

I went into our little laundry room and

carefully sorted the clothes. I reached into every pocket to be sure they were empty. Last time I did the laundry, I left a pen in the pocket of my shorts. The ink turned our wash into a humongous, blue-streaked mess!

I put a huge load into the washer, then headed over to the post office to mail my dad's present. As soon as I got home, I headed straight to the workshop. I looked at some of the characters that I'd painted on rocks, but Guthrie was definitely the cutest. I drew several possible designs for our shirts. My favorite was one with Guthrie standing with two baby camelpotamuses. The town's name swirled around them.

After my design was done, I put the clean clothes into the dryer and loaded up the washer again. Just as I finished, somebody rang the doorbell.

I ran to answer it and saw Andy grinning through the window. I pulled open the door and grinned back.

"How's it going?" Andy asked. "Have you worked on the design for the T-shirts?"

"Yeah," I said. "Come on in. I've finished a couple that I think will work. When are you guys going into L.A. to buy the shirts?"

"Well, the news isn't great," Andy said. "I just called the shirt place again to see how fast they could get them done. They want all the money up front before they'll even do the shirts."

"But we don't have the money yet," I said.

"Maybe you could talk to Carla's dad again," Andy suggested. "I'm sure he's cooled down by now."

"I doubt it," I said. "And I don't want him to slam the door in my face. Why don't we all just ask our parents to loan us $50? We can pay them back after we sell some of the shirts."

"That's a great idea, Megan!" Andy said with a grin.

"Hey, let me show you my designs," I said as I headed into the workshop.

"Could you grab the plane tickets, too?" Andy asked. "I'll put the tickets with the money in Dad's safe. That way we won't have to worry about losing anything."

"Sure. Just a minute," I called.

I picked up the designs, then headed to my room to find my purse. I unzipped the top and looked inside. The tickets weren't there. I turned my purse over and dumped everything onto my bed—and still no tickets!

Where could the tickets be? I wondered. I tried not to panic. I remembered dumping my purse out in the workshop to find my candy bar. Could the tickets have fallen on the floor? I ran back down to my work table and checked everywhere. There was nothing there.

I rushed back to the kitchen. "Here are the designs," I said. "I'll bring the tickets over to your place Thursday. I gave them to Mom to keep for me. And she's pretty busy right now. I don't want to bother her."

Andy gave me a funny look. Then he shrugged his shoulders. "Okay. Just don't forget them."

After he left, I went room to room in a frantic search for the tickets. I checked the closet. I dug through all the laundry, afraid I might have gotten the envelope mixed in with the clothes. I even checked every strange place that I could think of—the refrigerator, the garbage, and under my bed.

Get a grip on yourself, Megan. The envelope has to be here somewhere. It just has to. I brought it home yesterday, and it couldn't have walked away by itself.

I tossed in another load of wash, then hurried to the front of the shop. I tried to signal for Mom's attention and forgot to watch where I was going. I slammed right into a glass cabinet. There was a loud thud.

A customer looked in my direction to see where the noise came from. I grinned at her

50

to let her know that everything was all right. When she looked away, I rubbed my thigh. I knew I'd have a huge bruise. Oh, well, at least the bruise wouldn't be where the judges could see it.

Megan Steele, our last finalist of the evening, steps up to the microphone and shows us her outstanding bruises. Yes, if the Vargas School of Modeling and Self-Improvement can help Megan, it can help anybody. Sign up now!

"What is it, Megan?" Mom asked, pulling me out of my thoughts.

"Mom, have you seen an envelope from the travel agency?" I asked.

Mom shook her head.

"I had three plane tickets in the envelope," I explained. "I put the envelope in my purse right when I got it, and now it has completely disappeared. I can't believe it."

"I'll keep an eye out for it," Mom offered.

"Thanks. I also need another favor," I told her.

"Okay, honey, I'm listening. Go ahead," she said.

"You know the T-shirts that we're going to sell?" I asked her.

"The ones with San Angelo on them?" she asked.

"Yes. I know that once we have the shirts, they'll sell like hotcakes," I said. "But the problem is that we need to have all the money up front. So if we each borrow $50 from our parents, we'll have enough to buy the shirts and get started. We'll pay you back just as soon as we sell some of the shirts."

"You want to borrow $50?"

"I know it's a lot, Mom, but I'll pay you back right away," I said quickly. "We're not asking you to give us the money. We're planning to earn the money and pay you back."

"But what happens if the shirts don't sell for some reason?" Mom asked.

"Well, to make sure they do sell, Andy and I went to the newspaper this afternoon and told a reporter about our plan to get everybody plane tickets," I explained. "I told the guy about our car wash Saturday and Mr. Yokomura's offer to let us work at the Pizza Palace. He said he'd write a short story so people could help us if they wanted to."

Mom sighed. "Fifty dollars does seem like a lot, but you've certainly earned it, honey. I'm proud of the way you've worked so hard to get to the finals. Sure, the money is yours."

"Thanks, Mom," I said, giving her a hug. "You're the absolute best!"

*　*　*　*　*

As I walked into Andy's living room on
Thursday, I saw that Carla was already talking with Kate Zuckerman, Scott's mom. Carla
didn't even look at me. She was probably still
mad about slurping up Trish's facial.

Scott smiled as I sat down beside him on
the couch. I hadn't seen him or his mom since
I won the semifinals two weeks earlier. Kate
and Lucy, Andy's Mom, were close friends.
Lucy (we call her Mrs. G) had recommended
Carla and me to Kate for the Vargas Girl competition. Kate had agreed immediately to
sponsor us.

Scott seemed to get better looking all the
time. He had a dark tan, dark, curly hair, and
dark eyes. He'd been in a ton of TV commercials.

"How's my partner?" he asked. "How's the
Vargas Girl and soon-to-be star of commercials, TV, and movies?"

I glanced at Andy, who was glaring at Scott.
And Carla had her super-mad look on her face.
Whenever she's really mad, her eyebrows kind
of come together and her eyes narrow into
slits.

I laughed. "I'm nervous. It's easy for you to
be calm about the contest, since you're al-

ready Mr. Vargas. But I still have to face four other girls."

"We're all betting on you," Kate said. "Have you been working with Lucy?"

Both Lucy and Kate had taught me how to talk more clearly and present myself with more poise. We had practiced doing a lot of impromptu commercials, which meant I didn't get a chance to read my lines before I said them. I was supposed to be able to react confidently in any situation. I only wish it were true!

"No. We've been busy trying to earn money so all of my friends can go to New York to cheer me on," I explained. "It's going to take a lot for hotels and meals and everything."

"Maybe I can help a little," Kate said. "Scott and I keep an apartment in New York. Some of you can stay there instead of in a hotel."

"That would be great," I said.

Carla changed the subject. I guess she didn't want to hear any more about the contest. "Kate, do you have any commercials lined up for me?" she asked.

"I've had a couple that I think you could have done, but they were last-minute calls. You lived too far away to get there for the auditions," Kate told her.

Carla bit her lip. I knew she was disappointed. It suddenly occurred to me that maybe there weren't going to be any parts for Carla. Maybe Kate had lost interest in Carla after she was disqualified in the semifinals.

Would Kate drop me as a model, too, if I didn't become the Vargas Girl?

"Megan, I'd like to work with you and Scott this afternoon," Kate said. "I had the chance to watch two other finalists perform. I don't want to make you nervous, but you are up against some stiff competition."

"Well, they can't be as good as Megan is," Andy said confidently.

"I do think you have an edge," Kate said. "And Vicky Vargas definitely likes you. But we still have a lot of work to do."

I was surprised that Vicky Vargas liked me. She had every reason not to. I had spilled water all over her twice.

"I'm ready to work," I told Kate, "but there are a couple of things I have to tell Scott about. It'll just take a second."

"Go ahead," Scott said.

I told him all about the car wash we were having Saturday. And I filled him in on Mr. Yokomura's offer.

"Do you need some entertainment?" Scott asked. "For the pizza place, I mean. I brought my guitar to San Angelo with me."

"Wow! That would be great," I said excitedly. I glanced over at Andy. He didn't look thrilled about the idea at all.

"Are you sure you don't mind?" Andy spoke up. "We can't pay you, you know."

"I'd be glad to help out my partner here," Scott said as he touched my arm.

Andy looked away. I didn't know what to do. I couldn't be rude to Scott, but I didn't want Andy to be jealous. Why couldn't they be friends?

"Megan, could I have the plane tickets?" Andy asked.

How was I ever going to get out of this one? I'd practically torn my purse and the apartment apart looking for them. But I'd come up with zilch.

"Megan, I want to put them in Dad's vault before something happens to them," he urged.

What else could happen to them? I wanted to blurt out. But instead, I said, "I'll get them to you, Andy."

Kate stood up, signaling that it was time for Scott and me to get to work. Andy left, but Carla didn't budge. I figured she wanted to watch, so she could see me goof up. But after a few minutes, Kate politely told Carla that we needed to work alone. Carla gave me a dirty look as she walked out the door.

"Megan, I wish I knew some inside secrets about the finals," Kate said. "But Vicky has her own ideas on running a contest. She likes secrets and surprises. We'll just have to practice a little bit of everything."

Kate handed me a script. "Don't look at it yet," she said. "I want to see how well you do reading it cold."

Kate gave Scott a script, too, so he could help me practice. I stumbled over two of the tongue twisters. I decided to start over.

"No, Megan," Kate said as I started again. "You just keep on going. Have you forgotten everything that Lucy and I taught you?"

"I'm sorry. It's hard to concentrate," I admitted. I was worried about the tickets and about letting everyone down—especially Andy. He'd asked me to pick up the tickets, and I couldn't even handle that without a major disaster. How did I ever expect to win the Vargas Girl contest?

"Focus and concentration are most important," Kate said impatiently. "If you want to win, you must think only about the contest. Clear your mind of all other distractions."

I tried a few more lines, but I kept messing up.

"What's wrong?" Scott asked when his

mother left the room for a minute.

"I lost three airline tickets," I confessed. "I went to the travel agency and picked up the tickets. I remember putting them in my purse. But when I went to give them to Andy, they were gone. I keep trying to think of places where they might be."

"You'll find them," Scott said.

"I don't know. I've looked everywhere."

"Everything will work out," Scott assured me.

His mother returned and I did a little better at reading my lines after that. I guess telling somebody about the lost tickets helped. Kate kept us working right up to 6:00. By that time I was tired.

"I have to go now," I told her. "This is my week to fix dinner."

"All right, but I want you to spend at least two hours every day working with Lucy," she said.

"I will," I promised, even though I had no idea where I'd ever find even two minutes to spend with her. "And thanks for all your help."

I rushed home and cooked a big batch of chili. Mom and Trish seemed to like it. They both had second helpings. Then I hurried to the Pizza Palace to tell Andy about the tickets.

He was busy grating cheese when I walked in.

"Hi, Andy," I said as cheerfully as I could. "How's it going?"

"Great," he said sarcastically. "Just great."

Andy was using that weird voice that meant he was jealous. I knew most of the girls thought Scott was pretty special, but I thought Andy was the best. I wished he would realize that.

"So where's Scott?" Andy asked.

"I have no idea," I said truthfully. "Andy, quit worrying so much about Scott. He's not my type."

He shoved a pizza into the oven, then he turned to look at me.

"And what is your type?" Andy asked with a slight grin.

"Well, maybe he's someone like you!" I said and smiled.

He smiled back. I felt warm and happy all over. I decided to hold off sharing the bad news with him.

Andy pulled a finished pizza from the oven and cut me a slice. As he pushed the plate toward me, I looked into his eyes.

Somehow, the tickets didn't seem so important anymore. *I'll tell him soon,* I promised myself. *Very soon.*

Five

WE all got to the car wash early Saturday so we could set up our cleaning stations. Spud and Andy were going to soap the cars, Helen Mae and Carla would rinse them, and I'd clean all the windows. I guess everyone figured I couldn't get into too much trouble that way!

Chris and Scott were going to stand on Main Street and wave people in. Chris had made up two cute signs that they'd hold up. The signs announced, MEGAN MAKES THE BIG TIME! and LET'S GIVE HER OUR SUPPORT! I figured when the girls in town saw Scott standing there, they'd make their parents come to the car wash so they could ride along.

The car wash was packed in half an hour and stayed that way until it ended at noon. I'd been nervous that Andy was going to mention the tickets again. But since we were so busy, he hadn't had a chance.

I'd made it through most of the car wash without any major blunders. My only near catastrophe was Mr. Simpson, the high-school principal. I didn't notice that he was rolling down his window. I squirted a huge blast of glass cleaner all over his glasses and his shirt, but he just laughed. He thought it was a riot.

At noon, we packed up our supplies and headed home. We split up for a while and agreed to meet in front of the Pizza Palace at 3:30. Mr. Yokomura and Andy were going to show us how everything worked.

Within an hour, we were experts at grating cheese and slicing mushrooms, green peppers, olives, and pepperoni. Mr. Yokomura had already prepared the pizza dough in round, flat balls. He showed us how to flatten, punch, and knead the dough. Then he tossed the dough from hand to hand. We watched as the lumps of dough got flatter and flatter. As it spread out, Mr. Yokomura tossed each shell into the air. He made a real show out of catching the crusts and twirling them.

"You'd make a great Frisbee player," I told Mr. Yokomura.

"Don't let Megan try that," Spud said. "She'd have the pizzas all over the ceiling."

"I'll be doing the pizzas," Andy said. "Megan, you'll spread on the tomato sauce and put on the toppings. Then you'll put the pizzas into the oven for five minutes." He showed us how the oven worked. "The pizzas are super easy to cook, because they automatically go in one side and come out the other—all cooked and ready to slice. Spud, you do the slicing and clean the dishes."

Spud saluted. "Yes, sir."

Andy looked at Helen Mae and Carla. "The salad is all ready to serve. That's where you two can help, okay? And you'll also be our waitresses, of course."

Andy showed them where everything was and how much of the ingredients to use.

"Chris, you fill in wherever you're needed," Andy said. "But your official titles are cashier and busboy."

"Everything seems simple," I said to Helen Mae. "We shouldn't have any problems, right? Wish me luck. I can't afford to do anything klutzy tonight."

Helen Mae crossed her fingers for me. At 5:00, we all put on uniforms. We wore matching red-and-white pants and shirts. Andy, Spud, and I wore floppy, white chef's caps.

Mr. Yokomura left for a while and said he'd check in on us later.

"We're ready," I said. "Bring on the crowds."

I hoped that lots of people would come. The newspaper had done a great job of giving us publicity. I hoped business would be even better than Mr. Yokomura's typical Saturday night rush.

I had waited tables a few times. But working in the kitchen definitely was new for me. I thought of the pink icing disaster. I hoped I could handle putting pizzas together.

The first customers were a group of girls from our class. Scott sat on a high stool at one end of the room and began to play his guitar. The girls must have recognized him from commercials he'd done, because they started to giggle.

The girls ordered a pizza with everything. Andy kneaded and spun the dough until it was the right size, then placed it on a round, mesh tray. I carefully spread the tomato sauce around the top of the dough.

Andy laughed. "It doesn't have to be that perfect, Megan. You're not painting a picture. As business picks up, you'll have to move a lot faster than that."

"Okay, okay," I said. "Don't make me nervous."

I lifted gobs of grated cheese out of the bin. Half of it landed on the counter instead of on the pizza. I looked at Andy in exasperation.

"Don't worry about it," Andy said. "You're doing great!"

I instantly felt a little better. Andy always had that effect on me.

I finished the toppings and popped the pizza into the oven. Carla brought over two more orders. After a while, I got into a rhythm and it was pretty easy to keep up.

I took a second to check out the crowd. Business was booming! The place felt really homey and cozy. Scott was singing and people were laughing.

Things were going great—until Carla gave us an order for eight hamburgers.

"I don't know how to tell you this, Megan, but you're going to have to handle the pizzas solo for a while," Andy said. "I have to go fry some burgers on the grill. Yell if you need me, okay?"

I nodded and tried to give myself a pep talk. "Just do the best you can," I said out loud. I couldn't afford to do anything stupid to goof up this big night. Not in front of Carla and Andy and Scott. I'd never live it down.

As if she was reading my thoughts, Carla leaned over the counter. "Maybe you'd better let me do the pizzas," she said.

"I'll be just fine," I said.

"Okay," she said and left. Boy, Carla could make me so mad sometimes. I was really tired of everybody always expecting the worst from me.

I grabbed one of the rounds of dough and worked it just the way Andy had done. When I twirled it around, my finger went through the dough. I took a new round and started over. This time I did all right, and the dough fit into the round tray perfectly.

I quickly added the ingredients and handed the pizza to Spud.

Cooking wasn't so hard, after all, I decided. After I'd finished four pizzas, I felt pretty good. I even decided to be a little daring. I took the next round of dough and tossed it into the air, like Mr. Yokomura had done. I caught it on my fist.

"Hey, everybody," Spud yelled. "Come watch Megan."

I could have strangled him. A bunch of kids crowded around the counter. I tried to ignore them and concentrate on what I was doing. I'd done some baton twirling—this couldn't be any harder.

I silently counted one-two-three-TOSS. As I forced the dough up into the air, Scott hit a wrong note on his guitar. It clanged throughout the restaurant. The limp piece of dough sailed into the air, came close to the fan, and landed right back down on my fist. I gave Carla a proud look, and she turned away.

The crowd clapped and yelled. "More! More!"

I grabbed another piece of dough. I felt like I was on stage doing a play. Once I get into a part I'm doing, I get over the nervousness.

I pounded the dough, punched it, tossed it from hand to hand, spun it a couple of times to get it flat, then tossed it into the air again. This time the dough took off. It flew higher and higher. I raced around the kitchen, trying to predict where it would come down. It landed neatly across my outstretched arm.

"Megan! Megan! Megan!" the crowd chanted.

I did a few more orders, then Andy came back. "Boy, you were great, Megan," he said, as he pulled my chef's hat off. "Why don't you let me take over now?"

"Oh, let me do just one more," I pleaded. "I'm having a great time."

"Okay, but please be careful," Andy said.

I glanced over at him for a second to make a face and show him that everything was under control. I tossed the crust higher in the air than I had before. It felt like everyone in the place had grown quiet and people were anxiously waiting to see where the crust would come down.

"I've got it! I've got it!" I yelled as I ran across the kitchen and smacked into Spud. The pizza came straight down and landed with a splat on Spud's upturned face. He let out a muffled yell.

Everybody howled and clapped. Spud looked so funny with the limp pizza draped over his face.

"I've never seen Spud so quiet," a boy from school yelled.

"I'm sorry, Spud," I said, trying to control my giggles. "You shouldn't have gotten in my way."

"I'll get you for this, Megan," he sputtered as he tore the dough from his face. Then he ran out of the kitchen.

With Spud gone, I had to put the pizzas in the oven after I made them. We were getting so many orders that I was afraid we were going to get behind. I shoved the pizzas in the oven as fast as I could.

Suddenly, Andy screamed, "STOP!"

I couldn't figure out what was wrong. Andy brushed past me and flipped off the oven.

"Oh, no!" I groaned.

I saw that pizzas had splattered on the floor behind the oven. I had put too many in at one time and they were coming out the back end of the oven. I raced to the back and tried to catch a pizza as it fell. It was scorching! I dropped it on my toes, and the sauce coated the tops of my sneakers. I jumped back to get out of the way of another pizza and I skidded in the mooshy, sticky mess.

My chef's hat flopped over my face, and I was glad nobody could see me crying. Andy knelt beside me.

"Are you okay?" he asked softly.

"I'm so embarrassed," I mumbled tearfully. "I've ruined everything."

"No, you haven't. We'll get this cleaned up and be back in business in no time," he said.

Andy helped me to my feet, straightened my cap, and wiped my tears with a paper towel.

"Megan, you were the hit of the night," he said with a grin. "Helen Mae said people were ordering pizza just so they could watch you toss the crusts."

My other friends gathered around me, wanting to know if I was okay. Even Spud came in and began to help clean up the mess.

"Let's get back to work, kid," Spud said with a grin.

* * * * *

We all met back at Yokomura's the next morning to clean up. It didn't take us long to put everything back in order.

"Okay, gang, let's check out the figures," Andy said as he opened his notebook. "Mr. Yokomura gave us a break on the supplies. So we did even better than I thought we would."

"And what's that mean exactly?" Carla asked.

"Well, we made enough money from the car wash and from selling pizza to buy two more tickets," Andy said proudly. "Then we'll have to pay full price for the other two, since tomorrow's the cheaper fare deadline."

Oh, no, the tickets! I knew that I'd have to tell Andy what had happened. I'd stalled long enough. My luck had run out.

"Speaking of tickets," I said.

"Megan, did you bring them?" Andy asked.

I slumped down in my seat. "I...uh...can't find them," I mumbled.

"What?" Andy asked in disbelief.

"I said I lost the tickets," I blurted out.

"You what?" Carla yelled.

"Andy, why did you ever let Megan get her hands on the tickets?" Spud asked. "You know Megan better than that."

Even Helen Mae gave me a disgusted look.

"Are you sure they're lost?" she asked me. "Have you checked everywhere?"

I nodded. "Of course I have."

"I don't know how you can be so stupid," Carla said.

This time I couldn't argue with her. I didn't understand how I could be so stupid either.

"Megan didn't lose them on purpose," Scott said in my defense. "Give her a break."

"Yeah, you mean break her leg," Spud muttered.

"What are we going to do now?" Chris asked. "I wish I could get a hold of my parents and borrow some money from them. If they call home, I'll ask. But we can't count on it."

"Megan, I can loan you the money," Scott offered. "I'd have offered before when you told me about the tickets, but I was sure they'd turn up."

"Thanks, Scott, but I have some money in the bank that's supposed to be for college," I said. "I'll ask Mom if I can use some of it now."

I felt sick. Why did Scott have to mention that we'd already talked about the tickets? I thought that was our secret.

"Have you called the airline to ask about getting new tickets?" Andy snapped.

"Yeah, I did," I admitted. "They used to

70

give you new tickets for free. But now they charge you anywhere from $50 for each ticket up to the whole fare all over again. It's not fair."

Carla stood up and put her hands on her hips. "Why don't we just forget the whole thing?" she asked. "We put all this work into raising money and Megan messes it up. Maybe we shouldn't go after all."

"No, you guys have to come with me," I said. "I'll get the money somehow. I promise."

"Carla, you'll love the shopping in New York," Scott said to calm her down.

She didn't say anything, but I could see that she was calming down. Whenever Scott talked, Carla listened. That was for sure.

"Would you go shopping with me, Scott?" Carla asked.

"Uh, sure, if there's any free time," Scott said.

"My dad is taking us all out to dinner the night before the contest," I said. "Maybe you and your mom can join us," I said to Scott.

I noticed Andy's face and almost wished I hadn't invited Scott. But it would have been rude not to, since the three guys would be staying at the Zuckermans' apartment.

"That sounds like fun," Scott said.

Carla's face fell. I knew she wasn't interested in group sightseeing.

"I have to get home," Andy said abruptly. "And don't forget that we're going into L.A. tomorrow morning to get the T-shirts," he said to Spud and Chris.

Andy started to leave, and I followed him. "Can we talk a minute?" I asked him.

He glanced at his watch. "About what?"

"Come on," I said, leading him to a bench outside the Pizza Palace. "Andy, I'm really sorry about the tickets."

"Why didn't you tell me about the tickets before?" he asked.

"Because I kept thinking I might find them," I said honestly. "Are you mad at me?"

"No, I guess I'm just upset. You went to Scott and told him all about it. Why didn't you come to me first? I would've helped you look."

"I guess I went to him because it doesn't matter what he thinks of me," I said, looking at the ground. "But I do care what you think."

His face brightened, and he looked into my eyes. "Really, Megan?"

I smiled. "Yes, Andy, really. We just have to find a way to get new tickets," I said. "How could I possibly go to New York and compete without you by my side?"

"Don't worry. I'll be there," he said as he slipped his hand over mine.

Six

"MOM, is it possible to borrow some money from my college fund?" I asked her later that afternoon. I held my breath and silently willed her to say yes.

"Why are you asking for more money, Megan? I just loaned you $50. Is something wrong?" she asked.

"Tomorrow is the last day that we can get the cheaper tickets. And I need to buy three tickets," I explained.

"Isn't that why you had the bake sale and the car washes? And why you worked at Mr. Yokomura's?" Mom asked.

"Yes, we raised a lot, too. But remember when I asked you about my envelope? Well, I've looked everywhere, and it's never turned up. Everyone's mad at me for losing the tickets," I explained.

"Oh, Megan, why do these things always

happen to you?" Mom asked.

"I don't know. I have no idea what happened this time," I said honestly. "And that's why I need to borrow from my college fund."

"No, absolutely not," Mom said. "The college fund is in a special five-year savings account. If you take money out before the time is up, you get a big penalty."

"But, Mom—"

"There's no point in arguing, Megan. Unless you can find another way to get the money, the friends who don't have tickets will have to stay in San Angelo."

I knew I should tell her that two of the lost tickets were mine and Mrs. Gerritson's. But she was mad enough. I decided to ask my dad for the money instead.

I went into the kitchen and picked up the phone. I dialed and waited. But my usual bad luck appeared. Dad wasn't home. I tried off and on the rest of the day. I even tried first thing Monday morning, but he still didn't answer. I finally gave up. Dad hated to be disturbed at work, so I knew that calling him there was out of the question.

I sat at the kitchen table and watched the minutes tick by on the clock. I watched 5:00 come and go. The travel agency closed and the cheaper fare was gone.

I went across the street to the Pizza Palace to tell Andy my second bad news in two days. As I walked in, I saw that he was busy making a pizza.

"I'm sorry," I told him as soon as he saw me. "I couldn't get the money for the tickets I lost. I've let everybody down."

"Well, there's no use worrying about it, Megan," Andy said. "Things happen. We'll just have to earn more money."

"Thanks for understanding, Andy," I said. "I'll bet we do really well with the T-shirts. And I'll put in all my baby-sitting money and my allowance."

"Megan, I can't talk right now. I have some takeout orders to do," Andy interrupted.

I couldn't tell if he really was mad at me or not. Maybe he just had a lot of work to do.

"Sure," I said. "Sorry to interrupt. I guess I'd better get to the Bakers anyway. I'm baby-sitting for their kids tonight."

"See you later," Andy said.

"Bye," I said and walked out. Then I remembered that I hadn't even asked him about the T-shirts and about his trip into L.A.

Oh, well. I'd make it up to him later.

* * * * *

The T-shirts and my camelpotamus design turned out great. Most of the store owners in town agreed to sell some for us. Spud's parents sold some to tourists who stayed in their motel. And even Mom said I could display the shirts in our shop. I sold 20 shirts in three days.

One day Andy and Spud burst into our shop. Andy was holding up a newspaper.

"It's *The Los Angeles Sentinel*, Megan," Andy said. "Take a look at this."

My picture and article took up most of the front page of the lifestyles section. Everything was great except the headline: MEGAN THE KLUTZ MAKES GOOD.

"Oh, no!" I cried. "Why did she have to call me a klutz?"

"Why wouldn't she?" Spud asked with a snicker. "It seems pretty appropriate to me. Reporters are supposed to tell the truth."

"Read the article," Andy said. "It's good." I quickly scanned it and saw that the reporter had told how klutziness can be an asset— sometimes. Maybe it wasn't so awful to be a klutz after all.

The newspaper article really helped our T-shirt sales. We sold out our first batch of shirts and ordered more. At the end of the week, we all gathered in my living room to discuss the money.

"Well, we'd be in good shape," Spud said, "if Megan hadn't lost those three tickets."

I was probably going to hear about those tickets for the rest of my life. For what felt like the hundredth time, I said, "I'm sorry."

The phone rang and I ran to answer it. I was glad to get away from Spud's glares.

"Hello," I said.

"Megan, it's Dad. I just got your wonderful present. Thank you, honey."

"It's a camelpotamus. He won first prize at the fair," I told him. "I know a paperweight isn't much of a gift, not like what Trish sent you, but..."

"I had no idea you had this kind of talent, Megan. I'll sit it on my desk," Dad said.

"His name is Guthrie," I said softly.

"Guthrie?" Dad repeated. "Did you remember that was my dog's name when I was a boy?"

"Of course, Dad," I said. *I remember everything you tell me,* I thought.

"It's a perfect gift," Dad said. "But, honey, one present was enough. You really didn't have to buy me the others."

What was he talking about? Guthrie was the only gift I sent him.

"What do you mean, Dad?" I asked.

"You sent me three tickets to New York,

but I'm already here. I think you may have more use for them," he teased me.

"I can't believe it!" I screamed. "Oh, Dad, you have no idea how crazy it's been around here since I thought I'd lost the tickets forever. This is great news!"

"Everything's great?" Helen Mae asked as she walked into the kitchen.

"More than great! My dad has the tickets!" I said.

Helen Mae ran to tell the others.

"Sorry, Dad. I wanted to share the good news with my friends. Would you mail the tickets back to me?"

"Sure, I'll get them right back to you," he assured me. "I guess I'd better get going, honey. Thanks again for Guthrie. I'll be seeing you before long."

"I can hardly wait. I love you, Dad."

"I love you, too, sweetheart. Good-bye."

I hung up and rushed into the living room. "Did you guys hear the good news? The tickets aren't lost."

"I can't believe you'd mail tickets to New York," Carla said, shaking her head. "Megan, why do you do things like that? I just hope you don't do anything to mess things up during the finals."

I shot her a nasty look. I was used to her

snippy moods, but I wasn't going to let her ruin my chances in the finals. She'd had her shot at pushing me aside in the semifinals and it backfired on her. She'd better leave me alone now.

* * * * *

Between selling shirts, washing cars, and helping Mom in the shop, I worked with Mrs. G almost every day. I was as ready as I'd ever be. Let the contest judges throw out their toughest scripts. I was ready for anything!

We sold most of the T-shirts and paid our parents back. I could see that Mom was pleased about my keeping my word. I had paid her back—and fast. Things seemed to be going too well. It was making me nervous.

About a week before the finals, we were all hanging around Anderson's service station with nothing to do. It was strange to have some free time.

We were there for another car wash, but only two cars had come by all morning.

"Where are all the customers?" Spud asked.

"We've had a ton of car washes the past few weeks. I guess there aren't too many dirty cars left," I joked.

"I've got an idea," Spud said. "Let's borrow several of those leaf blowers and blow dirt on everybody's cars."

"You're nuts," Chris told him. "Besides, we almost have the amount of money we said we needed. Why don't we all just relax until we leave for New York?"

"I agree," I said. "I just want to say thanks to all of you for your support the last few weeks."

"Let's have a party to celebrate," Andy said. "We could have it outside. How about at the park on Monday?"

"Wait a minute," I said. "I think that's the day I have to baby-sit the Baker kids again."

"Maybe your mom or Trish would take care of them," Helen Mae suggested.

"I'll ask," I said doubtfully. "But Mom and Trish have been doing too much of my work lately. How about a different day?"

"I have to work right up to the day we leave," Andy said. "Monday is my only day off."

"Okay," I said. "I'll see what I can do."

*   *   *   *   *

It was hard for me to ask Mom about baby-sitting for me. I thought she'd get really mad about how much I was imposing on her. But instead she smiled and said yes.

I must have the best mother in the world.

On Monday, the Bakers brought their kids over to our apartment. The little one seemed crankier than usual. When I fed him chopped spinach, the little stinker blew the spinach all over my face and my new Guthrie T-shirt. I yelled and scared him. He started to cry.

Just then, Andy opened the door and peered in. He knew better than to laugh, but I saw his lips twitching.

"Are you about ready to leave?" he asked.

"You'll have to wait until I change. I don't look good in green, especially spinach green," I said. Mom took over watching the little one.

I hurried and changed into another Guthrie shirt. I was glad I had bought four. I walked back into the kitchen and whipped together my avocado dip for our party. Andy kept looking at his watch.

"I'm in charge of this party," he said. "I need to be there."

"Why don't you go on without me?" I suggested. "I don't want to hold you up."

"No, that's okay," he said quickly. "I'll wait for you."

Finally, we were ready to go. Andy took off at a run.

"What's the big hurry?" I asked, trying to keep up with him. "The other kids can get along just fine without us."

As we walked closer to the park, I could hear the town band playing at the pavilion.

"How come they're here on a Monday?" I asked. "I thought they played on weekends."

"Maybe they're rehearsing," Andy said.

"No," I said. "It looks like something's going on at the park tonight. Look at all the cars in the parking lot."

"Come on, Megan. "We're supposed to meet the other kids at the pavilion," Andy said.

As we walked closer, I saw that all the benches were full. "Hmm, I wonder what's going on?" I asked. "I haven't heard anything about a special program. Have you?"

Andy didn't answer. He just took my hand and pulled me toward the bandstand. Everybody turned to look at us and smiled.

"What's going on? Do I still have spinach on my face?" I asked.

"Don't you get it?" Andy asked grinning.

The band stopped in the middle of a song and began to play *New York, New York*. The crowd started clapping and calling out, "Megan! Megan!"

I looked around. I realized that nearly everybody was wearing our T-shirts.

"Andy! I can't believe this is all for me!"

"Carla's dad thought you should have a

send-off. What's the matter? You don't look too thrilled all of a sudden," Andy said.

I didn't know what to say. I was touched that the people in San Angelo would do this for me.

"Andy, I'm scared. Everybody expects me to win. What if I don't?" I asked. The pressure in my chest seemed to grow by the second. "I'm afraid I'll let everyone down."

Carla's dad was up on the bandstand. He signaled for the band to stop playing. "Megan, come on up here," he called.

After all my practice with Mrs. G, you'd have thought I wouldn't be nervous. But it seemed especially difficult to stand up in front of all the people I knew.

Andy gave me a little shove. "Go on, Megan. You're the only celebrity this town's ever had."

Most people fall down stairs, but I stumbled up them. Everybody clapped as if I'd done it on purpose. The whole town must have read the "MEGAN THE KLUTZ MAKES GOOD" article in the paper.

I stood beside the mayor while he told the crowd how I had made everybody proud. While he talked, I looked at the people in the front row. There were my mom and Trish sitting with the Baker kids. No wonder Mom had agreed to help me so quickly. She had known all about this.

I noticed Carla sitting there glumly. I knew she hated all the attention I was getting lately.

Mayor Townsend finally finished talking and urged me to say something to the crowd. I stumbled forward, nearly tripping on the wires that ran across the stage.

"Uh, thanks, everybody for coming here today," I began. "It really means a lot to me that you're behind me. Believe me, when I step up on that stage next week in New York, I'm going to be so-oooooo nervous! It'll help knowing that all of my friends in San Angelo are behind me."

Everyone cheered.

"And thanks for buying our Guthrie T-shirts. I hope you all like them."

There was applause as I stepped back. This time, I had gotten the wire tangled up with my sneaker. The tall microphone fell and banged the mayor on the chest.

He let out a yelp that echoed into the microphone and across the park. He jumped back and fell flat on the stage. I heard a few snickers and giggles from the audience.

I offered to help him up, but he glared at me. I guess the Townsends and I were going to have problems forever.

Seven

"ARE you all packed?" Mom asked me two days later. She was lying on the couch, sick with a fever and sore throat. She and Trish had both caught colds from the Bakers' baby. Mom looked terrible. And I knew she felt even worse that she'd have to miss my big moment in the spotlight. But I told her she had been a great help already.

"I think I have everything I'll need," I said, as I tied a big piece of string around a pizza box.

"Megan, why are taking pizza on the plane? They do serve food, you know," Mom said.

"Mr. Yokomura made it up special for Dad. It's his favorite," I explained.

I hurried into the bedroom to get my huge suitcase. I picked up my nylon dress bag that held the gown Trish had made for me. I had taken just about everything that was in my bedroom, except my panda bear. I decided that a finalist for Miss Vargas should be able to travel without her stuffed bear.

As I walked back into the living room, I remembered that I hadn't packed my sunscreen. I sure couldn't afford to get sunburned before the contest. I ran into the bathroom and grabbed a tube from the medicine cabinet. I opened my suitcase and shoved the sunscreen inside. As I closed the lock on one side, I saw that the sleeve of my favorite pink sweater was poking out.

I sat down on my bedroom floor and took a deep breath. I had to hurry, but I couldn't afford any screw ups. I glanced at the clock. The Rhodes' chauffeur was picking up all of us and taking us to the Los Angeles airport. Ten minutes later, I heard a horn honk. This was it! The next time I saw San Angelo I'd either be flying high as Miss Vargas or back to plain, old Megan. But I guess being Megan the Klutz had its fun moments, too—like at the town's celebration. Everyone had loved seeing Mr. Townsend lying flat on the stage. Everyone except Mr. Townsend and Carla, that is.

I ran over to my mom to give her a hug.

"No, honey, don't come close," Mom said, putting up her hands. "I don't want you to catch this, too. That's the last thing you need right now."

"Mom, I feel terrible that you and Trish aren't coming. You took care of the Baker kids for me, and you got sick," I said.

"Well, the celebration was fun. And, besides, if anyone had to get sick, I'm glad it was us and not you," Mom said.

"You've both been great, you know. The dress Trish made is beautiful. Maybe I'll ask Dad to take a picture of me on stage so you can see me in it."

"That would be great, honey," Mom said. "I'll be thinking of you. Please call and let us know how things are going, okay?"

"Sure, Mom," I said. "I will."

I ran down the hallway to Trish's room to say good-bye, but she was sound asleep.

"Bye, Mom," I said as I lugged my baggage outside. The chauffeur carried it to the trunk. "Wait just a second. I'll be right back."

I ran back inside. "Mom?"

"Yes, Megan?"

"Will you be disappointed in me if I lose?" I asked.

"Of course not. This is supposed to be fun for you. Enjoy being in New York with your friends. Don't pressure yourself so much. You know what happens when you get nervous,"

Mom said with a slight grin.

Just then, Trish walked in with a blanket around her shoulders. For once she didn't look so beautiful.

"Good luck, Megan," she said and sneezed.

"Thanks for making my dress," I told her. "You're the best sister in the world."

"Give Dad a hug from me," she said.

I bit my lip and turned away. But Mom noticed. "Honey, why are you nervous about seeing your father?" she asked.

"I...I don't know," I mumbled. I just was. Inside I felt that if I'd been a better daughter, he wouldn't have left us. But I'd never tell Mom that.

*   *   *   *   *

A loudspeaker squawked. *First boarding call for Flight 4213 to New York.*

We all hurried to get in line. Mrs. G was first, and I was right behind her. She gave her ticket to the man taking the boarding passes. I reached for my ticket—and panicked. My ticket! Oh, no! Where was it?

I fumbled in my purse. It wasn't there! Then my mind cleared and I remembered. I'd put it in the outside pocket of my tote bag so I wouldn't have to dig for it. I pulled out my ticket, nearly dropping the pizza. Leaving a trail of pizza sauce through the airport was all I needed right now.

As I grabbed tightly onto the pizza box, my purse fell off my shoulder. My coins and other junk fell under people's feet. I thought about leaving the stuff there and walking onto the plane without it. It'd be easier than facing my friends' grins and frustrated looks.

Yes, I was a klutz! So what? I wanted to scream.

Andy picked up my things for me and helped me zip up my purse. Spud pushed us forward.

"Come on, Megan. You're going to make us miss the plane."

Helen Mae, Carla, and I sat together. The three guys sat right behind us. Mrs. G had a seat right across the aisle. Carla insisted on having the window seat. Helen Mae sat in the middle, and I took the aisle seat.

I shoved the tote bag underneath the seat and decided to hold the pizza in my lap. I knew that, with my luck, if I put it in the overhead storage area, the pizza would fall splat on somebody's head.

I quickly read all the airplane safety instructions I found in the pocket of the seat in front of me. I was excited and nervous at the same time. This was the first time I'd ever flown. It was the first time for Helen Mae, Spud, and Andy, too. But they all looked calm.

"These instructions don't make me feel very safe," I whispered to Helen Mae.

"My parents say that airplanes are safer than California freeways," she said. "So stop worrying."

Once we were in the air, I relaxed some. I could see out the window a little bit. It was a weird sensation to be on top of the clouds.

Carla was wearing a headset that the flight attendant had given her. She had her eyes closed. I couldn't figure out why she had insisted on having the window seat if she wasn't even going to look outside.

Helen Mae and I talked about some of the things we wanted to do on Sunday. "I want to go walking through Central Park and see Greenwich Village," she said.

"Yeah, that sounds fun. I'd like to go to the top of the Empire State Building and see the Statue of Liberty, too," I told her.

I could hear Spud talking to the man across the aisle. I heard my name and nudged Helen Mae. "Hey, listen to Spud. This is a riot. He's actually bragging about me."

"You know all that stuff on TV about the search for the Vargas Girl?" Spud asked.

I couldn't hear the man's answer.

"Well, the Vargas Girl is sitting right in front of me. At least she will be after tomorrow night. My friends and I are going to be there screaming for her," Spud boasted.

"I don't believe what I'm hearing," I whispered to Helen Mae. "He does nothing but make jokes about me and now he's actually bragging. I'll never figure him out."

"Well, how can we all help but be proud of you, Megan?" Helen Mae asked. "This is pretty big stuff to be happening to us. And it's exciting to be included in it all—the money-making stuff and now your trip. I guess even Spud can turn into a nice guy if he wants to."

I glanced at Carla, but she was still listening to her headset.

"Then you don't think I have to worry about Carla pulling something to make me lose the contest?" I whispered.

Helen Mae shrugged. "I don't know. I guess I'd still keep an eye on Carla," she whispered. "You never know what she's thinking."

"I guess you're right. I don't want anything to go wrong this time," I said.

Soon, I felt my eyes closing. I'd been so nervous about the contest, the flight, and seeing my dad that I hadn't slept well in days.

For the first time in my life, I wanted something so much that it hurt to think about it. I really wanted to win. It seemed like everyone was counting on me. My family, my friends, my whole town. I didn't want to let them down. The flight attendant woke me up because she was serving lunch. My fingers were stiff from clutching onto the pizza box. Lunch tasted okay, but a few minutes later I felt sick. Mrs. G said it was airsickness.

I pushed my seat back into a reclining position. I closed my eyes and tried to will my stomach to calm down.

"Megan, are you okay?" Helen Mae asked. "No," I mumbled as the plane made a funny dip. It felt like a roller coaster when you fly down the first hill of the ride.

I kept my eyes closed and grabbed for the little pull-down table in front of me. I needed to hold onto something. I grabbed onto my food tray instead, knocking what was left of my barbecued beef sandwich onto my blouse and the pizza box.

"Ugh! Look at my blouse. The barbecue sauce looks really gross," I mumbled as the plane ride became smoother again.

People were staring at me. Some were even leaning into the aisle to get a better look.

"I could die," I whispered to Helen Mae.

"Just ignore them," she whispered back.

"I hope nobody thinks I'm with you," Carla said and looked out the window. I wanted to crawl under the seat.

The flight attendant helped me clean up the mess. She handed me a damp towel and I dabbed at my blouse.

I tried to sleep after that, but it was hard with Spud kicking at the back of my seat.

After a while the oniony smell on my blouse made me nauseous and I hurried to the restroom. There were several people waiting in line. When it was finally my turn, I ran inside, locked the door, and leaned against it.

I looked at my reflection in the mirror. Boy, was I a mess! My blouse was ruined. I tried cleaning off the dark stain with liquid soap and wet paper towels. But the more I rubbed, the wetter and soapier I got.

How could I face my dad looking like this? I had a jacket that would cover some of the stain, but not all of it. I was still dabbing away at my shirt, getting it wetter and wetter, when I heard somebody say on the loudspeaker that we had to go back to our seats.

I quickly slid the latch to open the door. I pushed, but nothing happened. I tried again. I moved the latch back and forth, then pushed. Still nothing. I rattled the handle. I kicked the door. Nothing.

In a panic now, I banged on the door and screamed for help.

"Please, somebody! Help me get out of here!" I yelled.

I stopped screaming to listen. Maybe somebody was yelling back. But there was silence.

Wasn't anybody out there? Weren't my friends worried that I hadn't come back to my seat? My wet blouse stuck to me and I shivered.

"Please, help me!" I yelled again as tears started rolling down my cheeks.

Eight

"JUST stay calm in there," a woman called. "The door is stuck."

I knew it wasn't my fault, but somehow I knew everyone would say that it was—especially Carla and Spud. I was tired of being Megan the Klutz. Why couldn't things go smoothly for once in my life?

"We'll have the door off the hinges in no time," I heard a man say.

I leaned against the door and waited. I hoped they would hurry. I didn't want to arrive in New York in a bathroom.

"I'm trying," I heard the man say. "The pins holding the door on are supposed to come right out. But one of them's really in there tight. I don't know if I can get it loose."

"We can't land until we get her out of there," a woman said.

Megan Steele arrives in New York with

*hopes of being the Vargas Girl. Her dreams
are shattered when she misses the finals
because she's locked in a bathroom. Long
after the contest ends, Megan is still waiting
and hoping that they'll set her free.*

"Megan, it's me," Mrs. Gerritson called
again. "Are you all right?"

"Yeah, I guess. Just get me out of here."

"You'll be okay, Megan," Andy called to me.

"You folks will have to go sit back down,"
someone said sharply.

I nearly went crazy waiting for them to get
the door open. When they finally did, the
flight attendant hurried me to my seat so the
plane could land. The other passengers gave
me dirty looks.

*Why didn't these things happen to other
people?* I wondered. I wished the emergency
door would open and I could jump out.

"I have to catch another plane," I heard a
man say disgustedly. "I hope I can still make
it before it takes off."

I ignored him and kept walking. I slunk into
my seat next to Helen Mae.

"Don't let those people bother you," she
said when she saw the look on my face.

"You'd think I got locked in the bathroom
on purpose. It wasn't my fault. When I tried
to push the door open, it wouldn't budge.

What could I do?" I asked her.

"Just tell me why these ridiculous accidents always happen to you," Carla said.

Spud bumped the back of my seat. "I'll bet nobody else in the world has ever been locked in the bathroom of an airplane," he said. "You know, Megan, someday you're going to be in the *Guinness Book of World Records* for the most consecutive dumb stunts."

"Cut it out, Spud," Andy said.

I was so nervous about everything that my hands were shaking. I tried to calm down, but I couldn't. I still had to face my father for the first time in more than a year. And I'd have to do it in front of everybody.

Finally, the plane was heading down to land. I put my seat straight up and closed my eyes. After the bathroom disaster, landing couldn't be too bad. The plane gave a couple bounces and then we were down.

I hung back, waiting until everybody else had left the plane. I didn't want anybody else to give me dirty looks. Spud and Carla were enough to handle. Helen Mae waited with me. To cover my messy blouse, I put on the heavy jacket Mom had insisted I bring.

"The last time I looked this bad, I was three years old," I told Helen Mae. "I got into my dad's oil paints and smeared them all over my hair, my face, and my new Easter dress."

"I don't think you look as bad as that," Helen Mae said. "Relax a little. Everything's going fine."

"Sure it is," I mumbled sarcastically. "A representative from the Vargas people is supposed to meet us. And I really wanted to look nice for my dad."

The world-famous jet-setter, Megan Steele, arrived from San Angelo today. As she stepped off the plane, she was a vision of loveliness in an elegant silk suit. Ms. Steele is known for her grace, charm, and wit...

By the time I walked off the plane, sweat was dripping down my neck. I clutched the pizza tightly and scanned the room for my dad.

"Megan, I'm glad to see you arrived safely." I looked up and saw it was Miss Vicky herself. Next to her stood Scott Zuckerman.

My new shoes had higher heels than I was used to. As I walked toward her, I stumbled over a piece of loose carpeting on the floor. I nearly dropped the pizza. I grabbed for it and it squashed against my chest. The box broke open, and sauce and anchovies oozed all over me.

I stood there like a zombie. I watched as Miss Vicky dabbed at the splatters of sauce on her beautiful outfit.

"Megan, I see you haven't changed," Miss Vicky said.

My face turned as red as the pizza sauce on my shirt. I remembered the two times I'd spilled water all over her.

"I'm so sorry," I said. "I wasn't expecting you to meet us at the airport."

"I wanted to make sure everything went right for you," she said.

Miss Vicky smiled at Mrs. G. "It's nice to see you both again. I hope you had a good trip."

"Yes, it was just fine," I lied.

Miss Vicky looked at me and smiled. "You certainly are a mess, Megan. Why don't you go clean up a little bit and then we'll go get your bags. I have a limousine that will take us to your hotel."

I quickly scanned the area for my dad, but he was nowhere in sight.

"I—uh—there are a couple of things I have to tell you," I said. "A few of my friends are with me."

I nodded toward the others. It was a bit awkward when Miss Vicky recognized Carla.

"Hello, Carla," she said. "I'm pleased to see you are here to support Megan."

For once Carla didn't seem to know what

to say. I actually felt a little bit sorry for her.

"My friends have been great," I said. "They've been working like crazy to earn the money for this trip."

"Yes, I know," Miss Vicky said. "Scott told me. He's come to take the boys back to his apartment."

"There's one other..." I started to say.

Andy poked my arm. "Listen, Megan. Someone's calling your name over the loudspeaker. I think you're supposed to answer that white phone over there."

"That must be my dad calling," I said excitedly. "He was supposed to meet me here."

I hurried over to the white phone.

"Honey, I'm sorry," Dad said. "I'm halfway between Boston and New York. My car broke down again. I have to get a tow truck to take it home for me."

"You'll be here for the contest tomorrow night, won't you, Dad?" I asked, feeling my stomach turn to knots. He had to be there.

"Don't worry, I'll be there in time. I'll fly down if I have to," Dad said.

"We could spend Sunday together, too—if you want to, that is?" I asked.

"Sure, honey, let's talk about it later, okay?" Dad said. "It looks like the tow truck's here now. You kids go on ahead and have dinner tonight. I've arranged everything at the Jade Dragon restaurant. You have a reservation for 8:00. Everything's paid for."

"Thanks, Dad," I said and hung up the phone. I was disappointed that he hadn't met my plane.

I walked slowly back to the group and told them what had happened. Carla and Helen Mae went with me to the restroom so I could clean up my shirt.

"Why didn't you tell me that Miss Vicky was meeting the plane?" Carla demanded.

"I didn't tell you because I didn't know about it," I said. "My dad was supposed to take us out. You knew that."

Carla started brushing her hair. She looked upset.

"Carla, I think Miss Vicki was impressed that you came with us," I said. "I know this must be hard for you."

"I don't know what you're talking about," Carla said. "What's the big deal?"

I just stared at her. Was she ignoring the fact that she was disqualified for ruining my dress? Maybe she was too embarrassed to think about it.

"You're right," I said. "It's no big deal."

We all got our suitcases and followed Miss

Vicky out to a huge white limousine. The air outside was so hot and muggy that it was hard to breathe.

"I feel as if I'm in a sauna room," I said.

A chauffeur helped us into the limousine. I was impressed. There was a huge TV, a refrigerator, and a full stereo inside.

"Wow, this is something," Helen Mae said.

I looked out the window and saw that people were everywhere. The sidewalks were filled with people walking in both directions. This city sure wasn't like San Angelo—or even Los Angeles.

Miss Vicky leaned her head back against the seat and closed her eyes for a minute. She was really glamorous, like the rich women on the nighttime soaps.

Scott had told us she had been a famous actress years earlier. Then she had started a line of cosmetics and opened up a whole string of modeling schools. Her latest project was a line of cosmetics for teens.

I dreamed about what it would be like to be rich and glamorous someday.

The multimillionaire, Ms. Megan Steele, just bought a movie studio, a TV company, and a chain of hotels. But even with all her millions, Ms. Steele never forgets her friends who helped her get to where she is today...

"Megan," Miss Vicky said, startling me. "You'll be meeting the other contestants this afternoon at 5:30. Mrs. Gerritson, I'd like you to be there, too. We'll go over some of the rules and procedures."

"Are the other girls here yet?" I asked.

"Yes, I met their planes earlier," Miss Vicky said. "They're all staying in the same hotel you are."

My hopes dropped. I thought that maybe Miss Vicky had come to the airport especially for me.

A few minutes later the limousine driver pulled up in front of a gorgeous hotel.

"If you have any problems, leave word at the desk," Miss Vicky said. "And try to get some rest, Megan. You look tired."

We thanked her and followed the bellhop up to the nineteenth floor. Our room was huge, and we had a great view of the city. There was a big basket of fruit on the desk.

Helen Mae ran around the room looking at everything. "Wow!" she said, bouncing on one of the beds. "This room is great!"

"It's not too bad," Carla said, trying hard to sound uninterested. "But the colors in here are pretty dull."

Helen Mae and I grinned at each other. Carla had to work hard to find something wrong with the room.

"So what'll we do first?" Carla asked. "Go shopping at Bloomingdale's? There's some time to kill before dinner."

"Dinner?" I asked, looking at my watch. "Oh, that's right. It's three hours later now. That seems so weird. Go ahead and do what you want to. I'm going to rest until the meeting."

I noticed that Helen Mae was staring at me. "Megan, you don't look very good. I hope you didn't catch anything from your mom and Trish."

"No, I'm okay. I'm just tired and nervous," I said, hoping that Helen Mae was wrong.

We are sorry to announce that Megan Steele has had to drop out of the Vargas Girl contest. She has been struck down by a terrible disease and is at death's door.

I had to laugh at myself. My crazy daydreams get out of hand sometimes. There was a knock on the door that connected our room to the next one. Helen Mae opened it and saw that it was Mrs. G.

"If you girls want to go shopping, I can show you around for a little while," Mrs. G said. "But I need to be back for Megan's meeting at 5:30."

I was a little disappointed not to be going with them, but it felt great to be alone for a while. After they left I rinsed out my blouse and unpacked some of my things. I took out my gown and checked it. There was no way that Carla could have gotten to it, but I wasn't taking any chances.

I set the little alarm clock that Mom suggested I bring with me on the night table. Then I stretched out on the bed. I kept thinking about my dad. I couldn't wait to see him. I wondered if he had changed at all. Or maybe he would think I had.

I woke up half an hour later and felt a little better. I saw that it was 5:15 already. I changed into white cotton pants and one of my camelpotamus shirts, then hurried to the Regency room. Miss Vicky and the other four contestants were already there.

"Come on in, Megan," Miss Vicky said. "Girls, this is Megan Steele from San Angelo, California."

The other girls and their chaperons smiled. As I sized up my competition, I realized that none of us was beautiful.

Miss Vicky went through some of the rules. "Now, remember that while you're here in New York, you're representing the Vargas company, so please act like responsible young women," she said.

No matter how many times we asked her,

Miss Vicky wouldn't tell us what we'd have to do in the contest.

Miss Vicky left us alone to get acquainted. The girls seemed friendly, and I liked all four of them.

There was Kimberly Aikens from Illinois. She looked older than the rest of us. She wanted to be a dancer.

Nicole Stevenson, from New York, seemed really relaxed about the whole thing. She wanted to be a model. Becky James, from Georgia, was the prettiest. She hadn't made up her mind whether she wanted to be a teacher or an astronaut. And Lisa Gray from some little town in Oklahoma hoped to be an architect. She couldn't get over some of the buildings in New York.

"And I'm from a small town in southern California," I told them.

"I love your shirt, especially the funny animal," Lisa said.

"Thanks. It's a camelpotamus. I did the design."

"Do you want to be an artist?" Becky asked.

"No, I'm not talented enough for that. Actually, I don't know what I want to be," I admitted.

"We're all getting together for dinner tonight," Lisa said. "We'd like you to come."

"I'd love to, but I have reservations for dinner at a Chinese restaurant," I explained.

"We're going to ask Scott Zuckerman to go with us. He's worked with all of us in the semifinals," Kimberly said.

"He's great, isn't he?" I asked. "I'm sorry to tell you this, but I've asked him to join me and a bunch of my friends from California. My friends came with me to cheer me on. And Scott's mother is my sponsor."

There was a long silence. Then Becky said, "That certainly gives you a big advantage, doesn't it?"

"I don't think so," I said honestly. He's not a judge and neither is his mother."

We talked a little more about the contest. We made guesses about what Miss Vicky would ask us to do. The more we talked, the more nervous I felt.

What was I doing here? I didn't have a chance. I was going to embarrass myself and the entire town of San Angelo. I just knew it.

Then I took a deep breath and straightened my shoulders. I might be a lot of things, but I wasn't a quitter. My friends were behind me. They had come all this way to support me. I had to go out on that stage and do my best—no matter what!

Nine

"WE can't all go in one taxi," Chris said to Scott. We had gathered in our hotel lobby to go to Chinatown. "I have extra money. I'll get another taxi."

"I'm going with Scott," Carla said.

Helen Mae, Andy, and I went with Chris. We all met again in front of the Jade Dragon. Even though it was almost dark, the air was still hot and muggy and I felt as if my clothes were sticking to me.

We walked into the restaurant. I usually get nervous in new situations, but I walked right up to the desk and asked if there was a reservation under my name.

"Yes," the hostess said. "You are Malcolm Steele's daughter, right? He called earlier. Everything has been taken care of. Please come this way."

She led us to a large round table in the

middle of the crowded room.

"Let's all order something different so we can try a little of everything," I suggested.

Besides my own order of Haang Yan Gai—chicken with almonds—I ordered enough fried shrimp and meat-filled dumplings for everybody.

After we ordered, we talked about our plans for the next two days.

"How are we doing on money?" I asked Andy.

"We're doing great so far," he said.

"Then let's go to Coney Island tomorrow morning," Chris suggested. "We can eat those famous hot dogs and go on some rides."

"It sounds great," Scott said.

"I can't go," I said. "I have to get my hair done in the morning. But maybe I can meet you at the beach afterward."

"What'll we do Sunday?" Spud asked.

"How do we decide? There's so much to see," Helen Mae said.

"How many of you would like to see a Broadway show?" Mrs. G asked. "I'll get tickets if you want to go. My treat."

Everybody wanted to go—except me. I wanted to see my dad.

"Can I let you know later?" I asked her.

It was hard for me to think beyond Saturday night. If a miracle happened and I won, how would my life change?

Spud began acting like a two-year-old, sticking his chopsticks in his ears and in his mouth. He looked like a walrus. I kicked him under the table.

"Can't you act like a human being for once in your life?" I whispered.

Instead of answering, he stuck his chopsticks in his nose.

"Spud!" Carla cried. "You're positively gross."

Just then the waiter set all the silver dishes of food on the table.

"Everybody dig in," I said. I tried to eat with chopsticks, but the food kept dropping back in my plate. "When my dad lived in San Angelo, we ate Chinese food a lot, but I never learned how to use these things right."

Chris was really good with them. He tried to teach Helen Mae, but she couldn't stop giggling.

"Hey, Helen Mae," Spud said, "you're as clumsy as Megan."

I had just used the chopsticks to pick up a dumpling, when Spud deliberately bumped my arm. The roundish dumpling tumbled down my leg and rolled across the floor.

I saw a man walking right toward it, but I

did know whether to scream in a restaurant or not. So I sat there and watched as the man stepped on it, skidded, and fell backward against a table. I held my breath. He waved his arms, trying to keep himself from falling. Finally, he gave up and landed on the floor with a thud.

Spud started to laugh. "Now, look what you've done, Megan," he said and stuffed a whole egg roll into his mouth.

"I've had it with you, Spud," I said. "You're always doing something to make me look stupid."

Without thinking, I dropped a dumpling right into his lap. I followed it with a couple of ice cubes.

I decided to let Spud see what it was like to be a klutz!

* * * * *

The next morning I had a hard time waking up. My alarm went off at 8:00, but my body still said it was 5:00.

The phone rang and Carla answered it.

"It's for you, Megan. It's your dad," she said, handing me the phone.

"Hi, Dad! Where are you?"

"I'm still at home, honey. I thought about

111

renting a car, but the shop said my car would be ready this morning. After I get it, I've got a couple of errands that I have to do before I can come down," Dad explained.

"I thought we'd have some time together today," I said, trying not to sound too disappointed.

"If the errands weren't really important, I'd be on my way to New York right now. Don't worry, honey, I'll be there in plenty of time for tonight," he assured me.

"If you're late, come right to the hotel ballroom. My friends will save you a seat. Andy will be watching for you, okay?"

"Sure, honey. I do hope to get there long before that, though," Dad said. "So how was the food last night?"

"The food was great," I said, "especially the dumplings."

I glanced at Helen Mae and Carla and they were giggling. I guessed they were remembering the look on Spud's face when I let him have it.

"Everybody said to thank you for the dinner," I told him.

"I just wish I could have been there," Dad said. "Well, I have to go pick up the car now. I'll see you later, honey."

As I hung up the phone, I sighed. "My dad

said he has some important errands he has to do," I explained. "He said he'll be down sometime before the contest."

Helen Mae and Carla got dressed and left to join the guys at Scott's. They were going to pack a lunch and come back for Mrs. G and me at noon.

I checked my dress again to be sure it was all right.

"Megan, what in the world are you doing?" Mrs. G asked.

"I'm trying to think of any way that Carla can possibly make me look stupid out there tonight," I said.

"Carla's not in the competition this time. Do you really think she'd try again to ruin your chances?"

"I don't know, but I guess I don't trust her," I admitted. "It's not a nice thing to say, but after what happened before..."

"Maybe you should try to be a little fairer to her, Megan," Mrs. G said. "After all, wasn't it you who made that sweet speech about friends meaning more to you than anything?"

Oh, yeah, that was me all right. I had totally messed up during the semifinals. And despite everything, my friends had stuck by me. I had stopped in the middle of the contest and thanked them in front of everyone.

"Yes, I meant that," I said. "But Carla didn't act like my friend when she ruined my dress, did she? Let's not talk about this anymore, okay? I'm just nervous. Let's work on tongue twisters some more before I go to the hairdresser."

"All right, but I wish you'd relax. This should be fun for you," Mrs. G said.

"I can't relax," I said. "Winning is important to me. My dad will be here..."

"Megan, your father will be proud of you whether you win or lose."

"I know, but I want everybody to see that I'm not a klutz. I can be good at things, too," I said defensively. "Even that stupid Los Angeles newspaper called me a klutz. I guess I've gotten really sick of it. I want to be known for something better than that."

Tears were rolling down my cheeks.

"It's only natural to be a little nervous," Mrs. G said. "But you can't expect this contest to change your whole life, Megan. Win or lose, you're still Megan Steele. And she is a very special girl."

Mrs. G gave me a hug.

"Now call your mom. Then we'll go down and have some breakfast. We can work on tongue twisters later, okay?" Mrs. G asked with a smile.

"Okay," I agreed.

*   *   *   *   *

I was expecting Coney Island to be like a Disneyland-by-the-sea. But it wasn't. There were no big, white beaches like we had at home. And the rides were smaller, too.

"Hey, let's eat," Spud said after a while. "I'm starved."

He spread out a blanket under the boardwalk and opened the big cooler they had packed.

"We made your favorite sandwiches," Spud said to me. "Tuna salad."

I couldn't believe it. Spud had been really nice to me ever since we got to Coney Island. Maybe dropping dumplings in his lap hadn't been such a bad idea.

"You'd better eat plenty," Carla said. "You'll probably be too excited to eat much dinner tonight."

I didn't say anything. I didn't want to discuss the contest with Carla.

"Scotty?" she asked, looking up at him. She had been flirting with him all morning. It was gross. "Do you have any idea what Megan will have to do in the contest?"

"No," he said bluntly. "And I couldn't tell

her if I did. It wouldn't be fair to the other girls."

"I think they're already mad at me because your mom is my sponsor," I said. "I guess they think it gives me an advantage."

I took a bite of my second sandwich. It had everything I liked in a tuna sandwich—eggs, celery, sweet pickle, and chopped olives.

"This is really good," I said. "Thanks for the sandwiches."

"Tuna salad was Carla's idea," Scott said. "To give you luck."

I smiled at Carla. Maybe I had been unfair after all. Carla and I went back too far to hold a grudge against her forever.

After we ate, we all walked along the boardwalk for a while. "Hey, who wants to go on the Cyclone with me? Megan?" Spud asked.

The thought of going on a roller coaster made me queasy. "Thanks, but I think I'll find a bench and just watch," I said.

"What's the matter?" Spud asked. "Are you scared?"

"No, I'm not scared," I said, scratching my arm. "I just don't feel very well all of a sudden."

"It's just nerves," Carla said. "Come on, let's have some fun."

Mrs. G looked at me closely. "Megan,

maybe you and I should get a taxi and go back to the hotel so you can rest for a while."

"I'll be okay in a few minutes. You guys go ahead."

"Are you sure?" Helen Mae asked.

"Yeah," I said. The others took off and Mrs. G and I sat down on a bench. I rubbed my back up against the wooden slats. "Ooh, I itch all over. A swarm of mosquitos must have attacked me."

"Your face is red and blotchy," Mrs. G said. "Maybe you got too much sun."

I shook my head. "No, that couldn't be it. I put on tons and tons of sunscreen."

All of a sudden I felt nauseous. I rushed to the nearest restroom and threw up. All I could taste was cucumber.

Cucumber! The sandwiches must have had chopped cucumber in them. And the strong flavor of fish had disguised the taste.

"Megan, dear, are you all right?" Mrs G asked when I came out of the restroom.

"No, I'm not. And I'm mad!" I said. "I was right about Carla all along. She did figure out a way to make me lose the contest."

"What are you talking about?" she asked.

Without answering, I pushed past Mrs. G and hurried over to the amusement park. Carla was just getting in line to buy a ticket for a ride. I grabbed her arm and spun her around.

"How could you do it? I'll never forgive you for this!" I cried.

"Never forgive me for what?" she asked, jerking her arm away from me.

The other kids had gathered around, wanting to know what I was yelling about. "This is between Carla and me," I said.

"You know I'm allergic to cucumbers. So you made sure there were some in the tuna sandwiches."

"I don't know what you're talking about. I never—"

"I don't want to hear any more of your lies!" I said. "You ruined my dress last time. And now you've found an even better way to ruin me."

I spun around and ran. I didn't want to hear anymore lies.

Ten

Back at the hotel, I looked in the mirror. "No!" I cried. "Mrs. G, look at me!"

My face and eyes were swollen and red. I itched all over and it was hard to breathe. I dug at my ears. They itched so badly I could hardly stand it.

On the way back to the hotel from Coney Island, Mrs. G stopped and bought some medicine to help the itching. It hadn't helped very much.

"Do you have special medicine at home for allergies?" Mrs. G asked.

"I don't know. I was a little kid the last time I ate a cucumber."

She picked up the phone. "I'm going to call your mother, then get you to a doctor."

Mom told her the name of the medicine that I'd taken when this happened before. Then Mrs. G handed the phone to me.

"Hi, Mom," I said into the phone.

"Sweetheart, what a rotten thing to happen. Did you forget you're allergic to cucumbers?" Mom asked.

"No, of course I didn't," I said. I explained about Carla and the sandwiches.

"Honey, I know it feels terrible right now, but the last time you were sick from cucumbers you were better the next day," she said.

That news didn't make me feel any better. The contest was tonight! After that, who cared how sick I was? It wouldn't matter anymore.

"I'll be okay," I said. "Mrs. G is going to get me to a doctor, so I guess I'd better go now."

"Okay, honey. I'll call later to see how you're doing. You do what the doctor tells you. Bye."

As I hung up the phone, there was a knock on the door. Mrs. G went to answer it. It was Carla and Andy.

"I don't want anybody to see me," I said.

"Carla wants to talk to you," Mrs. G said.

"Well, I don't want to hear any of her phony apologies!" I said as I ran into the bathroom and slammed the door.

I looked at the tub and decided that cool water might help to stop the itching. I filled the tub and climbed in. The cool water didn't help. I dried myself on one of the big, soft towels and put on a robe.

I slowly opened the bathroom door and peeked out. I wanted to be sure that Carla wasn't sitting there waiting for me to come out. There was no sign of her—or of Mrs. G. Maybe she'd gone to find the name of a doctor.

I stretched out on the bed and wondered why Carla would do such a mean thing to me. Ruining my dress was one thing, but making me sick on purpose was a lot worse.

Mrs. G came back a few minutes later. "I talked to the hotel manager," she said. "They're sending up a doctor to look at you and give you a prescription. He might give you a shot, too."

"I hope it helps. Nothing else has," I said, waiting for her to mention Carla. She didn't.

"Thanks for sending her away," I said softly. "I couldn't face her right now. I'm so mad."

"All of your friends were here," Mrs. G said. "They're worried about you."

"I'm sorry I spoiled their day at the beach," I said bitterly. "But now this whole trip has been for nothing. I'd better call the desk and leave a message for Miss Vicky that I'm dropping out of the contest."

"Wait until you see what happens when the doctor gets here," Mrs. G urged. "There's no use rushing into a decision about it."

"Mom said that the last time I ate a cucumber, I didn't get over it until the next day. That puts me out of the contest for sure."

* * * * *

I was amazed at how much the shot helped me. I wasn't itching as much, and some of the swelling in my face had gone down. I still couldn't hear or see that well, but I looked normal enough. With a little makeup and a curling iron, I decided that I might have a chance to win after all.

I went into the bathroom to get ready. I searched around for my toothpaste, but as usual it was nowhere to be found. I had to hurry, so I grabbed someone else's tube.

I squeezed the paste onto my brush and started to brush my teeth. Gross! It tasted awful! What kind of toothpaste did my friends use? I spit it out and rinsed my mouth. I squinted my eyes and read the label. It said, LADY ANNE'S HAND CREAM.

Hand cream? I spit some more, but I couldn't get the greasy taste out of my mouth. Mrs. G knocked on the door.

"Megan, the girls want to get changed for dinner. What do you want me to do?" she asked.

"Let them in," I said. "But I don't want to talk to Carla—now or ever."

When I came out of the bathroom, I avoided Carla's eyes. Helen Mae rushed over to me.

"I've been so worried. Are you okay?" she asked.

I smiled a little. There was no reason to be mad at my best friend. "I'm sorry for scaring you, Helen Mae. But I was pretty scared, too. Thanks to Mrs. G, I think I'm going to live."

"What about the contest?" she asked.

"I'm going to try. I don't want to let all of you down after you came all the way to New York."

Carla didn't say a word to me. I guess Mrs. G had told her that I refused to talk to her.

I was still lying on the bed when the others finished changing. "Aren't you going to get ready?" Helen Mae asked me. "We're supposed to meet the guys at the Savoy Regency Room here in the hotel for dinner."

I groaned. "I hate the thought of changing my clothes for dinner and then for the competition. I'll just skip dinner."

"Megan," Mrs. G said, "instead of going with the others, why don't you and I have room service bring us something?"

I liked that idea a lot. I didn't want people to be staring at me while I scratched.

When Carla and Helen Mae were ready to leave, Helen Mae came over to the bed and gave me a hug. "We'll be rooting for you. Just remember, no matter what happens, Megan, you're still the best! Okay?"

"Thanks, Helen Mae," I said. I tried to smile, but it was hard. "Be sure to save a seat for my dad."

At the door, Carla turned and looked at me. "Megan, I—"

I shook my head sharply and turned away.

"Good luck," Carla said so softly I wasn't sure that I'd heard her right.

I didn't answer.

* * * * *

As it grew closer and closer to the time to dress for the contest, I became even more nervous. I paced the room, stopping every few minutes to lean against a sharp corner of the closet to scratch the part of my back that I couldn't reach.

Part of me wanted to pick up the phone, call Miss Vicky, and tell her that I was dropping out of the contest. But a bigger part of me wouldn't let me quit. I realized that I wanted to do well not just for everyone else, but for myself. I wanted to know that I had given it my best shot.

Mrs. G put my clothes out across the bed. "I wish I had time for another bath," I said. "I feel hot and sticky."

"I brought some baby powder. Try that," she suggested.

The powder made me sneeze, but it helped a little. And pantyhose were the worst in hot weather. I tugged so hard that my toe went right through the silky material. I was glad that I'd brought two pair.

"Megan, before you put on your dress, let me see what I can do about your face," Mrs. G said.

I sat down at the dressing table. "It'll take a miracle to make this face look good," I grumbled.

Mrs. G used to be in the theater. She was great at performing miracles.

"Okay, ta da," she announced.

I looked up, and I couldn't believe it. She had done such a great job that I barely noticed the swelling around my eyes.

As she was helping me into my dress, the phone rang. It was my mom.

"Are you feeling better now?" Mom asked.

"I can see okay now, but I have trouble hearing. Mrs. G just made up my face, and I really don't look that bad. Please tell Trish that the dress is beautiful."

"I will," Mom said. "We just wanted to wish you well, honey. We're both sorry we aren't there with you."

"Me, too. Mom, please don't be too disappointed in me if I lose," I said.

"You know better than that, Megan. Just do the best you can," Mom said. "We're so proud that you made it this far."

I knew she was trying to make me feel better. I just didn't know if she was telling me the truth.

"I have to go now. I'll call you after it's all over," I said.

"Honey, it's only a contest. You're making this thing much too important," she said.

I knew she was right, but it was hard for me to think differently. I was scared. I was nervous. And I wanted to win. I wanted my dad to be proud of me.

I finished getting dressed. When Mrs. G and I were ready to leave, I took a couple of deep breaths. "Well, this is it. Thanks for all your help, Mrs. G. I would never have gotten through this awful day without you."

"I'm really proud of you for not backing out," she said as she gave me a hug. "Let's go."

We walked into the ballroom where the contest was being held. The room was huge, with two enormous chandeliers made of hundreds of tiny light bulbs. A huge stage took up one end of the room. Men were busy setting up rows and rows of chairs.

"There are only five of us in the finals," I said to Mrs. G. "How come there are so many chairs?"

"I guess Miss Vicky's staff will be here. And there will be plenty of media people to publicize the event," she explained.

"I wish I hadn't asked. Now I really feel sick," I admitted.

An usher told us to go directly to the dressing room on the left side of the stage.

The other four contestants and their chaperons were already there. I suddenly wished Helen Mae was with me, but only contestants and their chaperons were permitted in the dressing room. I was glad to see that the other girls looked nervous, too.

"Hi, Megan," Lisa said. "I love your dress. Did you get it in California?"

"Nope, my sister made it."

We admired each other's dresses and wished each other good luck.

"I've been looking forward to this night for weeks," Nicole said. "Now I'm so nervous I wish it was over."

We all nodded.

"I wonder if my dad is here yet," I whispered to Mrs. G. "I'm going out in the wings to see if he is."

I hurried out before she could stop me and peered around the edge of the red velvet curtain. The judges' table was all set up with pads and pens, silver pitchers full of water, and a microphone for Miss Vicky. The chairs were nearly all full, and everyone was talking. I saw that my friends were sitting together in the second row, but there was no sign of my dad. There was an empty seat next to Andy.

I hurried back to the dressing room. "My dad's not here yet," I said to Mrs. G. "I wonder what's wrong. Why isn't he here?"

"I don't know, Megan, but please stay calm. I'm sure he'll be here in time," Mrs. G assured me.

Kate Zuckerman hurried into the dressing room. "Megan, I got permission to come and see you. I just heard about your allergies. What brought on the attack?"

"Cucumbers."

Her hand flew to her mouth. "Cucumbers! Oh, no! You ate that tuna salad I made, didn't you? Cucumbers are my special ingredient. I always use them in the mixture!"

"You made it?" I asked. "I thought Carla and Spud made the sandwiches."

"They did, but I made up the tuna salad early this morning. I'm so sorry, Megan."

"Then Carla and Spud didn't even know there were cucumbers in it, did they?" I asked slowly. "Kate, Mrs. G, I have to go do something. I'll be right back."

"Megan, you can't leave now," Kate said. "Miss Vicky will be here in a few minutes."

"I have to go," I said. "This is really important."

I could feel the other girls and their chaperons staring at me as I ran from the dressing room. I ran down the stairs and over to where my friends were sitting. Andy and Helen Mae jumped up when they saw me.

"What's wrong?" Andy asked.

I ignored him and faced Carla. "I'm really sorry, Carla, for ignoring you. I thought you wanted me to lose, so you put cucumbers in our lunch. Kate just told me that she made it, not you."

"I tried to tell you, but you wouldn't listen," Carla snapped.

"She had every right to suspect you after the way you ruined her dress before," Helen Mae jumped in.

"No," I said. "It wasn't right of me to accuse her and not even listen to what she had to say. I am sorry, Carla."

"Don't let Carla kid you, Megan," Spud said. "She was trying to think of a way to get back at you for letting her eat Trish's facial stuff."

"Carla, I didn't know that was Trish's facial. Honest," I said.

"I admit I did think about getting even. I probably still will—sometime. But after we worked so hard to get to New York, I'm not stupid enough to ruin your chances of winning. What fun would New York be if everyone was mad at me?" Carla asked.

I knew that was the closest I'd ever get to an apology from Carla. I'd take it.

"Well, it looks like we both goofed up, right?" I asked.

Carla looked up at me then. "Good luck, Megan," she said. I think she even meant it.

"Mom's motioning to you from the wings," Andy said. "I think she wants you to get back over there."

I turned and waved to Mrs. G. "I'd better go," I said, looking at each of my friends. "Thanks, guys, for being here with me."

I ran toward the stage before they could say anything else. I didn't want to start blubbering like a baby.

Eleven

I rushed back up to the dressing room and got there just a second ahead of Miss Vicky.

Her gown was a shimmery, silver blue, and her diamond and sapphire jewelry didn't look much like the kind we sold in our store. Even in the hot room, Miss Vicky looked cool and elegant.

She chatted casually for a little while. I figured she was trying to calm us down. Then she gave us instructions about what was coming up next.

"You'll wait in here until your name is called. Once the first girl goes out and the contest begins, this door is to be kept closed. After each one of you is finished, go to the dressing room on the other side of the stage," she emphasized. "I don't want anyone to have an advantage by knowing what to expect."

I was almost glad that I didn't know what she had planned for us. It would only give me more to worry about.

"Any questions?" Miss Vicky asked.

My throat was too dry to ask anything. Miss Vicky smiled at us. "Don't look so nervous, girls. You have already been through the hardest parts. Tonight will be easy for you compared to the semifinals."

I'd believe that when it happened.

"Just remember, girls, you're all winners," she went on. "You have to be very special to have gotten this far. After the judges make their choice, refreshments will be served. I'm looking forward to meeting all of your families and friends. Now, good luck to all of you."

As soon as she left, I took another peek at the audience. The chair next to Andy was still empty.

"The contest is about to start and my father still hasn't shown up," I said to Mrs. G. "I wonder why he's not here. Maybe he's been in an accident or maybe he's sick. Maybe—"

"Shh," Mrs. G interrupted. "Megan, quit worrying. You are making yourself nervous. Your father is probably just held up in traffic. That's all. He'll be here."

"Will Ms. Kimberly Aikens please come on

stage?" an announcer called out.

I was glad the loudspeaker had interrupted my thoughts. The more I worried, the more I seemed to itch. Even my eyebrows itched.

Kimberly looked scared as she left the dressing room. I was glad that I wasn't first. My name was called third. Mrs. G gave me a quick hug. "You'll do just fine," she assured me.

I walked out onto the stage. I felt as if I couldn't breathe—and it wasn't because of my allergies. After going through all the preliminary contests, you'd think it would get easier, but it didn't. As I looked down at the audience, I suddenly felt really dizzy.

"Good evening, Megan," Miss Vicky said, and everybody clapped politely.

While she was giving some background about me—age, grade, where I lived, my sponsor, and things like that—I tried to see past the footlights. My father's chair was still empty. Miss Vicky said something to me that I couldn't hear. My ears felt as if they were swollen inside from all the itching and scratching.

"I'm sorry," I told her. "Could you repeat the question?"

"I just wished you good luck," she said. Everybody laughed.

Suddenly, a dozen people swarmed onto the stage. Some had notebooks, others carried cameras. They all began talking to me at the same time.

"Miss Steele, would you turn this way so I can get a picture of you?" one man asked.

I turned and a flash of light nearly blinded me.

"Megan, can I have your autograph?" a woman asked.

As I wrote my name, three other people were asking me questions. I felt as if I were being stampeded. I held up my hand. "Please," I pleaded, "one question at a time." I pointed to a young man to talk first.

"Ms. Steele, how does it feel to be the Vargas Girl?" he asked.

Then I realized what Miss Vicky was doing. Whoever won the contest would represent the Vargas schools to the media. The Vargas Girl would have to answer all kinds of questions.

"Well, I really haven't had time to take it all in," I said loudly so the judges could hear me. "It's the greatest thing that has ever happened to me."

"Do you use Vargas cosmetics?" a woman asked.

"I use very little makeup for every day," I answered. Then I remembered what Scott had said about the new teen makeup line. "But I intend to try the Vargas cosmetics made especially for teens."

Most of the questions were easy to answer, and I felt like I was doing well. Then a woman asked, "Don't you think these beauty contests make girls and women look stupid?"

I took a deep breath and hesitated, trying to think how I should answer. Suddenly, my back began to itch so badly I wanted to scream.

"The Vargas Girl contest definitely isn't a beauty contest," I said. "If it were, I sure wouldn't be here. The Vargas Girl should be a girl that anyone can relate to. She should be someone that people like right away. She should be natural, like your next-door neighbor."

I signed another autograph and answered a few more questions. Then a buzzer went off and the phony reporters and photographers left the stage.

During the interviews I hadn't had time to worry about my father. I looked out front and saw that he still wasn't there.

Miss Vicky stood up and walked toward me. "All right, Megan, I want you to do a commercial. It will be similar to one we will actually produce for television. You will be working with Scott Zuckerman."

Scott came on stage and gave me an encouraging smile. The commercial was like a little story. I was supposed to act very nervous and awkward. (So who had to act?) Then I had to show how the Vargas School of Modeling and Self-improvement helped me to become confident. Now *that* took acting!

Scott and I had to slow dance and read our lines from a teleprompter. I kept trying to look over Scott's shoulder to see if my dad was in the audience. I figured that I'd better give up. He'd never make it in time to see any of the contest. I began to wonder if he even wanted to see me at all.

Scott whispered in my ear. "Megan, sound like you're interested. Show some enthusiasm."

"Scratch my back," I said. "It's driving me crazy." He turned me around so my back was away from the audience. He tried to scratch it without anyone noticing.

"A little higher," I whispered.

"For Pete's sake, say your lines," he hissed. Mechanically, I read my lines. I didn't make any mistakes, I didn't have any disasters, but I knew I was doing badly.

I caught a glimpse of Andy and Helen Mae in the audience. They sat slumped in their seats, looking sick. I couldn't let them down this way. I couldn't let myself down this way. I had worked too hard to blow it all now—without even trying.

I tried to forget about my father and the rash. I tried to forget everything and concentrate on the commercial.

With every ounce of energy I had, I pushed myself to be excited and interesting. And I think I pulled off the best acting job of my life.

"That's more like it," Scott whispered.

As soon as the buzzer went off, signaling that my time was up, I rushed back to the other dressing room. I heard Becky's name called. She was the last one.

I sat down on a stool beside Kimberly and Lisa. Nicole sat in front of the mirror fixing her hair. Our chaperons were all seated in the audience.

"How'd you do?" Lisa asked.

"I did terrible on the commercial," I admitted honestly. "I couldn't concentrate."

"I hated those fake reporters and photographers," Kimberly said. "I didn't know what would be the right thing to say."

"It wasn't so bad," Nicole said confidently.

I tuned them all out after that. All I could think about was my dad and why he hadn't bothered to show up. I didn't know whether to be scared that something had happened to him, or to think that he hadn't cared enough about me to show up at all. After a whole year apart, he sure hadn't made any big effort to see me. What could have been so important this afternoon that it came before seeing me?

I was too upset to cry. Becky came back to the dressing room. All four of the other girls seemed excited. I knew I'd done well in part of the contest, but that wasn't going to be enough this time.

I hoped the judges would decide quickly so my friends and I could get out of here. We had one day left before we flew back to California. I realized that going home didn't sound so bad. I couldn't wait to be home with Mom and Trish and all my friends. Who needed a father anyway?

I picked up my brush and started running it through my hair. For the first time since I'd arrived in New York, I relaxed. I really didn't care about the contest anymore.

Just then the door flew open and there stood my dad. He looked exactly the way I remembered him. I stood there, not knowing whether to be mad at him or to run over and hug him.

As I looked into his eyes, I knew there was

no decision to make.

"Dad!" I said as I rushed into his arms. "Oh, Dad, I've missed you." I hugged him so tight I could hardly breathe.

He pulled away and looked at me. "I can't believe how much you've grown up in a year," he said with a big grin.

"I kept looking in the audience for you. What happened?" I asked.

"I got here just as you came on stage."

"But I never saw you," I said.

"I didn't want to interrupt everyone while I tried to find my seat, so I stood at the back until you were finished," he said.

My heart sank. "You saw everything? I was awful. When I didn't see you, I guess I didn't try very hard to win."

"Oh, honey, I'm so sorry I was late," Dad said. "But I had an errand to do."

Suddenly, I looked around and saw that the other girls were watching us. I knew that my dad wasn't supposed to be in our dressing room. But seeing him was really important to me.

"This is my dad," I said to them.

"Hello, girls. I thought you were all great. I'd hate to be one of the judges," he said.

They giggled at the compliment.

"I know I shouldn't be here," he said, "but

I thought I could sneak back here while the judges are making their decision. I wanted to give you this."

He handed me back Guthrie the Camelpotamus. "What's the matter with him?" I asked. "Don't you like Guthrie?"

"He's wonderful, honey. In fact, I thought he was so great that I entered him in a contest."

"What are you talking about?" I asked.

Dad reached into his pocket and pulled out a white ribbon. "You won third prize. I entered one of my seascapes in another category and only got honorable mention."

"What kind of contest was it?" I asked.

"It was a local competition for artists of all types. There was a special craft category. You beat out tons of people three times your age, honey."

I took the ribbon from him, but it wasn't the prize that was important. I couldn't believe that he had thought Guthrie was good enough to enter in a contest.

"But Dad, lots of people know you. Did I win just because I was your daughter?"

"No. I knew you'd ask me that, so I had a friend enter it. Nobody even connected the name Steele. You won it on your own. The judges were so impressed that they want you to enter your work next year."

I kept shaking my head in disbelief. "I never thought I had any talent—not like you and Mom and Trish. I wanted to win this contest so I could be good at something, too. I get sick of being known as Megan the Klutz all the time. People think it's funny, but it's not."

"Sweetheart, you're a wonderful artist, a wonderful girl, and a wonderful daughter," Dad said softly. "I loved seeing you up on that stage tonight. You're a very courageous young woman, Megan. Winning isn't always so important, you know. It's having the guts to get out there and try."

"Really?" I asked.

"Really," Dad said with a grin. "And you also have a whole bunch of friends out there who care about you a lot. That's a talent, too."

"I guess I never thought of it that way," I said.

"Making other people happy is a real talent," Dad said.

"You mean I make them laugh because of my klutziness?" I asked.

"People only laugh because they like you. People laugh with you, Megan, because you're so good at laughing at yourself. Quit being so hard on yourself."

The loudspeaker squawked and a garbled

voice asked, "Will the five contestants please return to the stage?"

We all wished each other good luck. This was it. All the work and all the waiting was almost over.

I tried to hand Guthrie back to Dad, but he said, "No, hold it for good luck." He kissed me and gave me a big hug. "Honey, I'm so proud of you."

Clutching Guthrie in my fist, I hurried to catch up with the other girls. We lined up on the stage. I saw my friends, Mrs. G, and Kate sitting in a row. My dad sat down next to Andy.

Miss Vicky stood up and the crowd quieted. "Before I announce the winner, I want to thank all five girls for being a part of this contest. All five are lovely, talented, bright young women," she said. "There are no losers here tonight. That I promise you."

I wriggled, trying to make the fabric of my dress rub against my itchy back.

"And now for the moment we've been waiting for..." Miss Vicky said in a dramatic voice. "I wish to present the Vargas Girl, Miss Lisa Gray."

The audience erupted in applause. The four of us took turns hugging Lisa. "You'll be great," I said, and I meant it.

Lisa was crying, and the others were bravely trying not to show their disappointment.

I looked down at my friends. They were all clapping politely. I could see the looks on their faces. They looked like the world was ending, but I realized that I felt great. In fact, I felt better than I had in a long time.

I looked down at Guthrie. He was supposed to bring me luck in the contest, but he'd turned out to be better than luck. He had made me realize that I did have special talents of my own—and not just as an artist. I had the talent of making people laugh. And that didn't sound so bad.

I waved to Dad and my friends to show them that I was really okay. Maybe losing out to Lisa was a good thing. Now I would have time to spend with my friends and family.

As I pulled my arm back down to my side, the rock slipped out of my fingers. It bounced on the edge of the stage and plopped right in Miss Vicky's silver water pitcher. Most of the audience started to laugh.

I groaned. I looked down at my dad and my friends and they were grinning. I grinned back.

Yes, Megan the Klutz was here to stay!

About the Author

ALIDA E. YOUNG and her husband live in the high desert of southern California. She enjoys writing novels and credits herself with being the inspiration for *Megan the Klutz*.

"Once, I sprayed my husband's shirt with window cleaner instead of spray starch," she says. "Another time, instead of using hair spray, I spritzed my hair with deodorant. I used to perform in plays, and many of the things that happened to poor Megan, happened to me."

Novels have long been a fascination of Alida's. "I think I was about ten when I decided to read every book in our library," she recalls. "It took me three years just to get through the *A*s. It was then that I decided if I ever wrote a book I'd change my name to Aaron Aardvark so my book would be the first one on the shelf."

Other books by Alida E. Young include *The Klutz Strikes Again*, *What's Wrong With Daddy?*, *Why Am I Too Young?*, *I Never Got to Say Goodbye*, and *Is Chelsea Going Blind?*